Legacy

a novel by

Jacquelin Thomas

D1564907

Legacy © 2017 by Jacquelin Thomas

Limited Edition

ISBN: 978-1543002232

In honor of my Ancestors,
Your struggles were not in vain

A Special Note from Jacquelin

Legacy was born out of my love for African American history. Although I am a contemporary writer, I have always wanted to try my hand at writing historical fiction as well. I loved writing this story because I was able to combine the two genres along with stories from within my own family vault.

Please note that the Yellow Fever epidemic in New Orleans actually took place in 1853. For the purpose of my story, I moved it up to 1838. Also, there is some debate whether *Quadroon Balls* or *Plaçage* contracts actually took place during the 1800's. These dances are rumored to have served a meeting space where free young women of color, guided by their mothers, charmed their way into the hearts and pockets of Louisiana's white males.

Debutantes were accompanied to the balls by their mothers, and when a white gentleman found a particular girl attractive and wished to take her in *plaçage*, he had to negotiate the terms with the mother, who often insisted on housing and that any children conceived by the union be recognized and educated. While some view this arrangement as prostitution; others choose to believe that these mothers sought to ensure that their daughters would not be left without some type of financial security.

I hope you will enjoy this story as much as I enjoyed writing it.

Enjoy...

Jacquelin Thomas

Prologue

June 1874

A single bullet fired from a six-shooter revolver entered Henri Toussaint's body, instantly stopping his heart. That same bullet managed to shatter Gemma's own heart into a million little pieces without striking her flesh.

She heard Henri make a gurgling sound as his body sagged, crumbling to the dirt.

Screaming, Gemma dropped to her knees beside him, cradling his head between trembling hands. "*Oh, mon Dieu, non...*" She didn't care about the expensive purple dress she was wearing.

A half dozen or so New Orleans's citizens surrounded her.

She sobbed, her shoulders shaking as tears streamed down her face. "*Non... non...*"

Blood pooled on his chest.

Gemma brushed her wet cheeks with the back of her hands. Then, for the first time since she'd knelt by his side, she looked up. Francis, Henri's younger brother, held out his hand to help her stand.

In her grief, Gemma blinked back tears and whispered, "Who did this? Why would they kill him?"

"I don't know, but I need you to listen to me. I'll take care of Henri. You should go home."

"Non. I'm not leaving him."

"Listen to me," Francis stated. "Go home. I'll come by as soon as I can."

"We should turn this over to the law."

Silence.

"If you won't do it, then I will," Gemma uttered. "As his wife, I will demand it." She stared at Francis for a long moment before noticing that everyone in the crowd was watching her.

"*Marriage de la main gauche,*" he said in

a low voice. "Left-handed marriages carry no weight. Only his legal wife can make such demands of the law. Now go home. I'll get some men to help me move my brother."

She made an audible sigh. "I will go home. Thank you for taking care of Henri."

Gemma's mind drifted back to her wedding day, just six months ago. She clutched the string of pearls around her neck, his wedding gift to her. They had been so happy together.

Although it was not considered a legal marriage, Gemma meant all of the promises she'd made to Henri and he to her. The color of her skin was fair, but that one drop of blood from her African ancestors made Gemma unworthy of marriage to a white man an impossibility in Louisiana.

Tonight, she'd planned on telling him that he was going to be a father.

He would never get to know the child she carried, the thought causing a lump in her throat.

Chapter 1

"I'm here to see Eleanor Blakemore."

"*Mrs.* Blakemore is not seeing anyone this morning."

Myra shook her head. "Girl, if you don't move out my way, I will chew you up and spit you out like tobacco. I mean it. I'm not leaving here until I see Eleanor."

"Hattie, it's fine," a voice called down from the spiral staircase. "Please take her to the library."

"Yes ma'am."

"If you knew what I know… you wouldn't be working for this woman," Myra said, following the young woman in the starched black uniform.

"Mrs. Blakemore… she's good to me. She's a nice Christian lady."

"Humph. If you say so…" She ran her fingers through her medium brown, shoulder-length curls.

Dressed in a pair of expensive looking pants and knit top, Eleanor strode into the room with purpose. "Thank you, Hattie."

The housekeeper left, closing the door behind her.

The two women glared at one another.

Eleanor spoke first. "I can't say that I'm surprised to see you."

"My granddaughter's getting married," Myra announced, ignoring the comment. "I want her to wear the Toussaint pearls when she walks down that aisle. The way you turned your back on this family—you don't deserve them."

"They're all I have of my mother. I'm keeping them."

"They belonged to *our* mother, Eleanor. I know you want to pretend otherwise, but you're just as black as everybody else, even though the color of your skin and them blue eyes tell a different story."

Eleanor released a long sigh. "You and I are the same complexion and we share the same eye color. The only difference is that you've chosen to live in a black world and I choose to live in a white one. I don't hate you for your choice. Why not give me the same courtesy?"

"My choice didn't mean turning my back on my entire family. Your own husband don't know he's married to a black woman. Wonder what he'll do if he finds out?"

Eleanor's eyes narrowed. "Are you threatening me?"

"I want the pearls—they belong with the *Toussaint* family—a family you no longer claim. All the women in our family should've worn them on their wedding day. I was robbed of that legacy and so were my daughters. *No more.* Belva is my first granddaughter to marry and I intend to see that necklace around her neck."

Eleanor pulled a checkbook from the desk drawer. "Here, I'll write you a check. Use it to buy your granddaughter a pearl necklace."

"I don't want your money—I *want* the Toussaint pearls or I'll go down to that law firm and tell Mr. Winston Blakemore, III all about your lil' dark secret."

"They're not here. I keep them in a safe deposit box at the bank."

Switching her purse from one shoulder to the other, Myra stated, "You got twenty-four hours to get me them pearls. Unless you want these fancy painted walls to start crumbling down all around you, *Mrs.* Blakemore."

"Happy Birthday, Myra. You look good for sixty-six."

"Maybe you haven't heard, but black don't crack."

Myra sat in her car a moment before turning the ignition. A week ago, to the day, she thought she'd seen a ghost when Eleanor walked out of that restaurant. Initially, Myra considered that it couldn't possibly be her sister because she had been presumed dead for so many years. But when their gazes met, she saw the truth.

Eleanor was four years older than her. She'd disappeared the day their mother had been found dead. Myra always believed that whoever killed her, had also taken her sister.

She all up in that house acting white, Myra thought with disgust. *Thinking she better than the rest of us.*

***

"Nana, where have you been?" Belva asked when Myra entered the house. "I was getting worried when you didn't answer your phone."

"Honey, I'm fine. I had to run a quick errand." She surveyed her granddaughter's toffee-colored face, noting the dark circles underneath her eyes. "Are you getting enough rest. You look tired."

"It's the wedding. There's so much to do. I feel like I'm not getting anywhere with the planning."

"You hired that expensive wedding planner—let her do her job, sugar. I don't want you running yourself ragged."

Belva waved off her concern. "I'll be okay, Nana."

Her granddaughter had been living with her since she came to New Orleans to attend Dillard University. She currently worked with a bank as a data analyst and was engaged to her college sweetheart Vincent Moreaux, who was preparing for law school.

They gathered in the family room where

Myra pulled out a photo album. She opened it and said, "This was my mother, Daisy, on her wedding day."

She was so beautiful."

Myra murmured, "I think so, too." Her mother's smile was a smiling rosy flower and her head was capped by a mass of bronze-gold curls.

"You see those pearls around her neck? Those are the Toussaint pearls. They've been in our family since the 1700's."

"Really?"

Myra nodded. They were given to my great-great-grandmother, Gemma in 1874. You know… you look a little like her."

"Do you have any pictures of her?"

"I have this one right here."

"Is this her husband?"

Myra nodded. "This was her first husband, Henri. He was very much in love with her, and she loved him, too, but they weren't able to marry back then. Besides, Henri already had a wife and daughter. My granny told me that Gemma met Henri at one of them *fancy* balls, but I don't know if that's really true."

"Mama told me about the Quadroon Balls,"

Belva stated. "She told me how mothers basically sold their daughters as sex slaves to these men for houses, money and slaves."

"I'm sure they didn't look at it quite that way," Myra said. "I can't imagine taking part in something like that, but I believe that those mothers only wanted the best for their children. We can only imagine how our ancestors suffered at the hands of some of those slave owners."

"Nana, who is this little girl with you?"

Myra had never really talked about Eleanor with her children and grandchildren. "That was my sister."

"Oh, she's the one who died... That must have been so hard for you. Britt gets on my nerves, but I don't know what I'd do if something ever happened to her."

"It was a terrible time for me," Myra admitted. "I'd lost my father, then almost a year later, I lost my mother and my sister at the same time."

"I can tell that you still think about her," Belva said. "I can see the sadness in your eyes."

"Well, I have no reason to be sad anymore. We have a wedding coming up. I thank the

Lord that I've lived long enough to see you walk down the aisle."

"I'm glad you're here, too."

"God's blessed me with six beautiful grandchildren. I hope to be around long enough to see each one of them grow up and do great things."

"Nana, you are going to be around for a long time," Belva stated. "You eat healthy and you exercise. You're probably in better health than I am."

"I doubt that," Myra said with a soft chuckle.

"I guess I'm just selfish. I don't want you to ever leave me. I need you, Nana."

Myra took one of Belva's hands in her own. "Child, you don't need an old woman around. You're starting a new life with your handsome young man and you've got your mother. One day you'll have your own children and I'll be a distant memory."

Belva shook her head. "You will be more than that, Nana. You've poured so much into my life—not just my life, but my mom and her siblings… all the grandchildren. You will live on in all of us."

She touched her granddaughter's cheek. "You have such a sweet spirit."

"Now, tell me more about these people. I love hearing our history."

Myra smiled. "We're blessed to have all these albums and family records. So many families have gaps in their history, but ours have remained pretty solid. I hope that it remains this way."

"I intend to make sure," Belva stated. "I will keep our history when you no longer can, Nana. I promise."

Eleanor paced her living room floor, while praying that Myra would keep her mouth shut.

I knew it was a bad idea to come back to New Orleans. If only Winston had listened to me.

She had no idea whether Myra would still be here—Eleanor left home when she was fifteen years old and hadn't seen her sister until last week. They'd run into one another at a restaurant in the French Quarter. Now the witch was trying to blackmail her over a string of pearls. Eleanor was reluctant to part with them because they were the only link to her family that she would ever have.

I'll just have to find some that look exactly like them and give them to Myra. It's not like she'd know the difference. She was only twelve when I left home. She won't remember them.

Eleanor picked up her car keys. "Hattie, I'm going out for a while," she said. "Please make sure all of the bathrooms are spotless. We have guests coming over for dinner this evening. The caterers should arrive by five."

"Yes ma'am."

She spent her afternoon searching for a necklace that closely resembled the one Eleanor had in her possession. She had no intentions of giving up her mother's pearls. They meant more to her than she could put into words.

Myra called them the Toussaint pearls, but they could've been a gift from her maternal grandmother to their mother. No one knew for sure. She searched her memory to try and recall if Granny ever mentioned them.

They never spent that much time with her because her mother said that the woman never really liked her. She blamed Daisy for everything that was wrong in her stepson's life.

Eleanor knew that her father had abused drugs. In the end, they'd both died because of it.

She shook the memory from the forefront of her mind. She didn't like to think of her parents in that way. Instead, she preferred to believe that they were in heaven, living out the lives they had been robbed of on earth.

Chapter 2

"Mama, how did things go with Eleanor?"

"Julia, it's not gonna be as easy as I thought," Myra responded. "She doesn't want to give them back." She'd confided in her daughter that her sister had been found alive after all these years. After seeing Eleanor, Myra discovered that she was the wife of Winston Blakemore III. She googled her and found a photo of her sister wearing the pearls.

"Why not?" Julie sank down on the sofa beside her mother. "It's not like she's a part of this family."

Myra agreed. "I basically threatened to go

to her husband and tell him the truth about her."

"Would you really do that?" Julia asked. "Could you do that to your sister?"

"What sister?" Belva asked. "Nana has another sister?"

Neither one of them had heard or seen her enter the room.

Myra gestured for Belva to join down.

"Belva, I recently found out that my sister didn't die like we thought. She's alive."

Her eyes sparkled with joy. "Nana, that's wonderful, but why didn't you tell me? We were just talking about her. When do we get to meet her?"

"It's a bit complicated," Myra said.

"In what way?" Belva wanted to know.

"Eleanor has embraced her whiteness. She doesn't want to associate with folks like us… black folks."

Belva looked from her mother to her grandmother. "Are you serious?"

"Yeah, I am."

"Have you talked to her?"

"Belva, I went to see her earlier today. Remember, I told you about the Toussaint pearls?"

When she nodded, Myra continued. "Well, she has them. There was a picture on the Internet of her with them around her neck. I want you to wear them on your wedding day."

"They're beautiful," Belva murmured. "It's nice of her to let me wear them on my wedding day."

"You don't understand, sweetie. I want the pearls returned to *this* family. She is no longer apart of *this* family, so Eleanor shouldn't have the necklace."

"Nana, I don't want you worrying about those pearls. I can buy a nice necklace to wear."

"You *will* wear the Toussaint pearls," Myra stated. "I'm not letting that woman keep a family heirloom."

"How could such beautiful pearls cause so much trouble?" Belva wondered aloud.

Her mind temporarily strayed from them as she fought a wave of dizziness. She struggled to maintain her composure so as not to worry her mother and grandmother.

For the past couple of months, she'd been feeling awful but decided to keep it from everyone. Belva didn't want anything to put a shadow on her wedding to Vincent. She pushed away from the table. "I think I'd better head out. I'm supposed to meet with the planner in an hour."

She stood up.

Belva felt the room spinning.

Alarmed, she reached out. "Mama ..."

Julia was instantly beside her. She led her daughter over to the couch in the family room, and asked, "Honey, what's wrong?"

"Nothing," Belva lied. "I think I'm just really excited. I love Vincent so much and I can't wait to become his wife." Fanning herself with her hand, Belva continued, "It's so hot in here."

"It's June," her grandmother pointed out. "It's always hot this time of year. You have to stay hydrated in all this heat."

"Honey, I'm going to get you some water."

Julia returned with the water. "How are you feeling, sweetie?"

"I-I don't know. I feel so hot and so... so weak..."

Belva fell to the floor in a slump.

Reaching for Julia, Myra comforted her daughter. "Sweetheart, Belva's going to be okay.

She just got over excited, that's all. She's always been very fragile, you know."

"Lord, what's wrong with my child?" Julia whispered as they waited for the paramedics to arrive.

Myra released a sigh of relief when they showed up minutes later. She stayed out of the way as they rushed in and immediately went to working on Belva.

"We need you, Lord," she whispered. "Please don't let nothing happen to my granddaughter. This family's been through enough loss for this year." Myra thought of her husband who died a little over a month ago. Three months prior to his death, they lost their only son to a motorcycle accident. "I can't take no more right now. I can't."

Julia rode with Belva in the ambulance while Myra drove her own car to the hospital. It gave her time to be alone with God. She prayed from the moment she got behind the wheel until she pulled into the parking lot of Ochsner Medical Center.

Myra parked and rushed through the emergency room doors. She met Julia in the lobby.

"We just lost Daddy and Jared. I can't lose

my daughter."

"Everything gonna be fine," Myra said, trying to reassure Julia. "Most likely, Belva been stressing herself over this wedding. She's lost weight—I don't think she really eating like she should."

"Yeah, I've noticed the weight loss, too. I thought maybe she was losing intentionally."

"I'd planned to go back home tomorrow, but I can't leave now," Julia said. "I need to call Mike." She lived in Jackson, Mississippi where her husband, Michael Simone, taught at Piney Woods School, an African American boarding school.

"You should let Vincent know as well," Myra interjected. "I think he and Belva had plans this evening."

Myra sat down in a nearby chair while her daughter searched for privacy to make her phone call.

Vincent arrived half and hour after Julia called him, followed by Theresa, Myra's youngest daughter.

Belva was taken for tests.

Julia and the doctor spoke for a bit, then she joined her family saying, "They've ordered some blood work and some other tests to see what's going on."

"So they think it's more than stress?" Myra asked.

"I guess they're trying to rule out everything else."

As soon as Belva was settled into a private room, she was allowed visitors. Three at a time, so she let Julia, Vincent and Theresa visit with her. Myra wanted to be last. She had no intention of just saying hello and leaving.

Belva's eyes were closed when she entered the room. When she spotted her grandmother, she tried to sit up. "N-Nana?"

"Sssssh, lay back down, sweetie. Get some rest."

Belva held up her left hand. "Where's Vincent?"

"He's right outside. Do you want me to get him?"

Belva shook her head no. "He's not mad, is he?"

"That man adores you, Belva. He's not going to be upset with you for not feeling well— if he is, then he's not the man for you." Myra brushed aside Belva's bangs, away from her eyes.

"You're right, Nana."

"Now lay back and close your eyes. Get all the rest you can. I know you want to start your marriage right." Myra gave a little laugh. "My memory can sometimes fail me, but I can clearly remember passion."

Belva broke into a smile. "Nana, I'm surprised at you. You won't even say the word, *sex* out loud."

"Hush now," Myra murmured. "There are some things a person just shouldn't talk about." Her eyes strayed briefly toward the closed door.

Belva chuckled. "Nana, can you tell me the story behind the Toussaint pearls and why they mean so much to you?"

"You don't want to hear about a necklace, child. I'm just being sentimental."

"Tell me anyway. It'll help keep me calm while we're waiting on the doctor to come back with results of the tests they took. I feel like I've been here forever."

Myra settled back in her chair. "Let me see... I guess the best place to start this story is when I was twelve years old. That was when my life changed forever..."

***

Tears filled her eyes and spilled down her face, grief and despair tore at her heart. A sensation of intense sickness and desolation swept over twelve-year-old Myra. Her mother's funeral was less than an hour away.

Her father gone... now her mother... and Eleanor was nowhere to be found. She had no one. She was a little girl facing the harsh realities of loneliness. She put a fist to her mouth to keep from screaming. She struggled to maintain her composure—she had to be strong her grandmother told her.

"Myra..."

She turned around at the sound of her name.

A woman stood in the doorway, dressed in black. Myra had never seen her before, yet she felt there was something familiar about her. "Hey," she murmured.

"Beloved, you will never be alone," she told Myra, her accent heavy. "Your ancestors watch over you. Our God watches over you."

"But He took them all away from me. How

can God love me and do this?"

The woman took Myra into her arms. "We may not understand why God allows such pain, but know that He will never forsake you. His angels watch over you, little one."

"Are they watching over Eleanor, too?"

"Yes, Beloved. They watch over her."

"Did you know my mom?"

"I knew your father and I want you to know that he is at peace. Your mother, too."

"Where are you from?"

"Senegal."

"I've never met anyone from Africa," Myra blurted.

"Beloved, during your lifetime, you will meet people from many cultures. You're going to see some amazing things happen, but you must never forget the past."

Myra didn't understand what this woman was trying to tell her.

"It's time to go. You need to say goodbye to your mother." She paused to let Myra lead the way to the front of the house where her grandmother and other family members had gathered.

"I was just about to come looking for you,"

her grandmother said. "Come here, baby."

She hugged Myra. "Granny loves you so much. I know you hurting pretty bad right now, but we gon' get through this together."

Myra looked over her shoulder to find the African woman who'd come to her room to talk with her, but she was gone. "Where's she go?"

"Who?"

"The lady from Africa," Myra stated. "She knew Daddy."

She felt her grandmother's body stiffen. "Do you know her, Granny?"

"Yes, I believe I do. She's probably gonna meet us at the church." Rising to her feet, she said, "We best be going ourselves."

The service for her mother was a simple one. Myra looked across the aisle to the empty pews. She had overheard her grandmother request that they be available for her mother's relatives, but no one had come.

Myra had never met anyone on her mother's side of the family. The only thing she knew about them was that they weren't black. She knew this because her parents had explained the harshness that might come because of her parents mixed race marriage. Myra couldn't understand why her maternal grandmother hadn't come to say goodbye to her daughter.

After the service when everyone had gone, Myra joined her grandmother in the living room.

"I looked for the African lady but I didn't see her."

"She was there," her grandmother murmured. "I could feel her presence."

Myra frowned in confusion.

"Baby, I'm just rambling." She pointed to a photo album under the coffee table. "Pull that out for Granny. I want to show you something."

Myra did as she was instructed.

Her grandmother opened it.

"Those pictures look so old," Myra commented.

"That's because they are… this is our family history documented. We have pages torn from old family Bibles where they recorded the births, deaths and marriages of our family. We are proud of our history. One day, all this will belong to you and I want you to pick up where I leave off."

"I will," Myra said, although she still didn't really understand.

"Do you recognize this woman?"

She stared at the strange looking photograph. It wasn't paper like most of the other ones, but it was the woman in the picture that captured her attention. "That's her," Myra exclaimed.

"Ziraili," her grandmother murmured.

"*Ziraili*," Myra repeated.

"Her name means God's helper." Tears welled up in her Grandmother's eyes. "If you met Ziraili, then I know everything's gonna be alright, baby. We gon' be just fine."

Chapter 3

Eleanor sat across from her husband in Restaurant August. It was nice to have a night out on the town. She loved the food served in this place, especially the banana pudding.

"Winston, do you really like it here?"

"In New Orleans? Yes, I do. Why?"

"I don't know. I miss Baton Rouge. Our friends."

"Honey, I think you should get out more. Meet some new people. Since we've been here, I noticed that all you seem to do is read. I know you received an invitation to join the Women's Club here. Why haven't you?"

Their waitress brought their food to the table, sparing Eleanor from having to answer her husband's question. She glanced at him, noticing that Winston was staring across the room. She followed his gaze to an attractive woman sitting at another table.

Eleanor cleared her throat noisily.

Winston turned his attention to her. "You okay?"

"I'm fine," she responded, her tone terse.

He gave her a puzzled look.

Ignoring his questioning gaze, Eleanor blessed her food, then picked up her knife and fork. She sliced into her chicken.

Throughout the course of dinner, Winston looked bored despite her efforts to include him in their conversation.

An hour later, Winston paid the check and they walked out of the restaurant.

"I know we've been married a long time, but do me the favor of pretending to enjoy my company," Eleanor said. "And respect me by not gawking other women while we're together in public."

Winston and Eleanor walked to their car. She snatched the keys from Winston saying,

"I'll drive."

"What's with the attitude, Eleanor?"

"I'm tired of being humiliated by you. You spent most of the evening watching some woman at another table."

"I thought I recognized her from somewhere," he responded, opening the door to the passenger side. "Let me drive. You're upset over nothing, so just calm down."

Eleanor got in, while Winston walked over to the driver side.

"You know that you're the one I love, sweetheart," he said as he turned the ignition. I'm telling you the truth. That woman looked familiar and I was just trying to figure out where I knew her."

Eleanor didn't believe him. She hadn't been blind to Winston's affairs since the day they left Baton Rouge.

They were on their way the door of their former home when she received a phone call from a young woman who claimed to be involved with Winston.

"Mrs. Blakemore, I know you think you've won, but you haven't."

"Excuse me? Who is this?"

"This is the person Winston was going to divorce you for," she sniped.

Eleanor laughed. "Oh, you poor dear... it's pretty clear to me that if what he told you was true—he has had a change of heart. Now be a good little pet and go off somewhere to pout. I'm sure the next married man is just around the corner."

She ended the call and the conversation.

For a brief second Eleanor closed her eyes, savoring her resentment toward her husband.

She still loved him, despite her broken heart. She had invested too much into this man and she wasn't going to just walk away with nothing. Eleanor intended to bide her time, which is why she never mentioned that conversation to Winston.

Eleanor's eyes grew wide as she realized that a vehicle had driven through the red light. She turned to her husband for a brief second, blinded by bright lights. They were in the path of an SUV. It was coming directly at them.

As it neared the passenger side of their vehicle, Eleanor screamed.

***

Winston opened his eyes. His gaze strayed to the window and the sunlight drifting into the room. There was a variety of strange and new sounds all around him, a low murmuring of voices, the steady beeping of a machine, random clicks and a low hum.

He blinked his eyes, trying to adjust to the brightly lit up room. He was in an unfamiliar place.

A face he did not recognize loomed suddenly in his view, then disappeared as quickly as it appeared.

Confused, Winston turned his throbbing head to the side.

The face belonged to a woman dressed in a nurse's uniform. She checked his IV.

He was in a hospital. But why?

"Eleanor…" He murmured groggily. He felt sleepy.

Winston struggled to fight through his confusion. His brain was foggy and not working properly. He drifted in and out of consciousness so nothing was making much sense.

He fought to remain awake while the nurse talked to him, but it was a battle that he was rapidly losing.

The next time he opened her eyes, Winston noted that it was dark outside. His friend and partner from the law firm entered the room.

He was still trying to piece everything together. "What happened?" Winston touched the bandage on his head, the movement causing him great pain.

"You were in an accident but you're going to be fine."

"Where's Eleanor?" he managed to get out. "Where—" Winston stopped short as memories of the what happened resurfaced.

The nurse was instantly by his side. "I want you to just concentrate on getting better right now."

He couldn't the dull ache of foreboding. Winston had a strong feeling that his friend was hiding something from him.

"What aren't you telling me?" he asked, fear spreading through his body.

He avoided eye contact with Winston.

"Charles," he prompted. "Where is my wife? I need to see her now."

A doctor entered the room, followed by a nurse.

"Calm down, Mr. Blakemore."

A wave of fear swept through him. "Where is my wife? Is she okay?"

"Your wife..." the doctor began. "She sustained trauma to the head. We did everything we could but she is in a coma..."

Winston tried to focus on the doctor's words despite his growing panic. He noticed the nurse injecting something into his IV. He hoped whatever it was—it would stop the pain brewing in the pit of his chest.

Myra brushed Belva's hair. "There you go, baby."

"Thanks Nana. I don't want Vincent seeing me with my hair all over my head. Can't scare him like this until after the wedding."

They laughed.

"Mama's bringing me a scarf to wear while I'm in here."

Myra touched her granddaughter's hand. "You okay, baby?"

Belva nodded. "It is what it is… I have leukemia, but I'm not going to let it stop me from living. I'm going to beat this cancer."

"Our God can do *anything*. The world may not have a cure, but He does."

"Preach Nana…"

"Girl, don't you get me started up in here. I get excited when I think about what a mighty God we serve."

Belva turned on the television.

"Accident last night… Prominent attorney Winston Blakemore III and his wife… critical condition…"

Myra's eyes grew wide. "Turn that up, please."

Julia entered the room, carrying a tote of things for her daughter. "Good morni—"

"Ssssh…" Myra interjected. "There was a bad accident."

Belva gave her mother details while her grandmother listened to the news report.

"I need to check on Eleanor," she said. "I'm going to check and see if she's at this hospital."

Julia nodded in understanding.

Myra grabbed her purse and heading out of the room. She walked to the nurse's station.

"Can you check to see if there's an Eleanor Blakemore here? I heard she was involved in an accident last night."

"Yes, she's here."

"Thank you," Myra said.

She rushed down the hospital hallway holding a bag close to her body and whispering, "Father God, please give me strength and wisdom in Your word. I need You Lord. My sister needs You. She needs You now."

Myra went to the nearest information desk. "I just found out that my sister and her husband were brought here. Her name is Eleanor Blakemore. I need to see her."

"Yes, she's in room 3401."

"Thanks," she uttered before racing toward the elevator.

Myra paused a moment outside of her sister's room. "Give me strength…"

She opened the door, her eyes traveled to the pale woman in the hospital bed, tubing and tons of machinery attached to her body.

A nurse entered the room.

"How's she doing?" Myra eyed the ventilator. "Has she been awake?"

"No ma'am. If you'd like, I can have the

doctor come in and talk with you."

"Please… this is my sister."

A few minutes later, a man strode into the room, saying, "Mrs. Madison, I'm Dr. Brady. I understand you are the patient's sister."

"I am," Myra stated. "Where is Winston?"

"He's two doors down."

"Is he okay?"

"His injuries were minor."

Myra glanced over her shoulder to where Eleanor lay. "She looks so fragile."

The doctor gave her a sympathetic smile. "She sustained an injury to the head in the accident. She's in a coma."

"Dear Lord…"

"The good news is that your sister can continue to heal while in the coma."

Myra's eyes filled with tears. She quickly wiped them away. "Is it okay if I sit with her for a moment?"

"I always encourage people to talk to coma patients. They recover faster when they hear the voices of loved ones."

"Thank you, Doctor."

The steady beeping of one machine unnerved her, so Myra struggled to block out the sound.

Opening her bag, Myra pulled out her Bible and sat it upon Eleanor's body. She anointed Eleanor's body with oil and prayed for healing. When Myra was done praying, she read Scriptures aloud to her sister.

"Don't you give up, honey," she told Eleanor. "I don't know if you can hear me or not, but if you can—you just hold on. Trust the good Lord to give you strength. God is not a liar and you can trust His promises."

"Who are you and what are you doing in here with my wife?"

Myra turned around to face Winston. "I came to see Eleanor."

"How do you know her?"

"I've known her a real long time, Mr. Blakemore."

"That's impossible. We only just moved here a few months ago." He moved closer, his gaze never leaving Myra's face. "Are you two related?"

"We are," she stated. "Eleanor is my sister."

"Oh, I'm so sorry for my reaction." He paused for a moment, then said, "I never knew she had a sister. She told me she was an orphan."

"We've been separated for a long time." Myra chose her words deliberately. "We ran into each other recently."

She could tell from the expression on Winston's face that Eleanor never mentioned anything about her family to him.

He offered her his hand. "I'm Winston Blakemore III."

"Myra Toussaint Madison."

"It's nice to meet someone from Eleanor's side of the family."

Myra look over at her sister. "They said she's in a coma, but that she can hear what's going on around her. Do you think that's true?"

"I'd like to think so."

Her eyes traveled to the bandage on his head. "Looks like you need to be laying down yourself."

"I needed to see Eleanor."

"I understand."

"How did you find out about the accident?" Winston inquired.

"My granddaughter is in this hospital and I was visiting here. It was on the news."

"Were there any…"

Myra shook her head. "The driver in the other car suffered some minor injuries. If they had been speeding…" She didn't bother to finish the sentence.

A nurse entered the room, greeting them.

Myra noticed Winston's attention and his gazed stayed longer than she liked on the young woman caring for his wife. Folding her arms across her chest, she said, "I hope you don't mind my visiting Eleanor."

"No… not at all. Spend as much time as you'd like with her."

"Thank you, Mr. Blakemore."

"Call me, Winston. We're family."

She gave a tiny smile. "I'll give you some privacy with your wife. I need to get back to my granddaughter."

Chapter 4

Julia rose to her feet when her mother entered Belva's hospital room. "How is she?"

"As well as can be expected," Myra whispered. "She's in a coma."

"Mama, I'm so sorry."

They kept their voices low, so as not to disturb a sleeping Belva.

"I met that husband of hers and I don't like him one bit. He's a womanizer. You should've seen the way he was eying the nurse—the very woman caring for his comatose wife."

Julia shook her head in disgust.

"He asked me how I knew Eleanor."

"*Mama, what did you say?*"

"I told the truth. I told Winston that Eleanor and I are sisters."

"Oh Lord…"

"Calm down, the man don't know that I'm black. The same way he don't know his own wife is a black woman."

"It's not your job to spill Eleanor's secret, Mama."

"It's not my job to cover it up, either. Julia, I'm not trying to ruin my sister's life. I'm more concerned about losing her again. I'm angry with her, but I want her alive. If it comes down to saving her—I don't care who knows the truth."

Eleanor was in a dark space. She heard, but could not respond to the soft, murmuring voice.

Fear knotting inside her, she sat huddled in a corner. Eleanor had no idea where she was, the place smelled of familiarity and unfamiliarity at the same time, the silence thick and almost cloying.

Someone was calling her name.

Eleanor opened her mouth to speak, but no sound would come forth. The voice continued to call out to her, urging her to say something.

Whatever this place was—it was terribly dark. She never liked to be in the dark because it reminded her of death.

Eleanor closed her eyes, wrapping her arms around her legs. She wouldn't move—she would stay here until somebody came to save her.

The next day, Winston was discharged. He was waiting on the nurse to return with the paperwork.

A tall, slender woman with dreadlocks and skin the color of smooth chocolate entered the room. "I had to come see you. I heard about the accident and I was worried."

He smiled. "This was probably not the smartest move, sweetheart."

"You're a criminal attorney and I'm the District Attorney. People will just assume we're colleagues." She moved closer to the bed. "Although we're much more than that."

She bent down and kissed him. "I was so worried about you."

"I'm fine. Eleanor got the worse of it."

"Is she going to be okay?"

"We don't know."

"Were you drinking that night?"

Winston shook his head. "I only had one glass of wine. That was it."

"You never saw the other car coming?"

"I had a green light. It wasn't until I was in the middle of the intersection that I realized the car wasn't going to stop." After a moment, he added, "Eleanor was upset and I was trying to calm her down."

"I hope she recovers quickly."

"Thank you, Janet."

"In the meantime, what about us?" she asked. "I'm sure you need time to focus on your wife's care."

"She has a sister I didn't know about," Winston stated.

That peaked Janet's attention. "Really?"

He nodded. "Apparently, the two ran into each other recently. I just don't know why Eleanor never bothered to mention it to me."

Janet smiled. "Well, it's not like you're telling her everything."

He kissed her.

A noise interrupted them.

Winston looked up to find Myra glaring at him.

"I knew you were good for nothing," she uttered. "My sister down the hall in a coma and you in here with this woman."

"There's a lot you don't understand about my marriage to Eleanor."

"We can agree on that."

Janet grabbed her purse. "I'd better leave."

"It would be a good idea," Myra said.

"Wait a minute…" Janet uttered and paused in her steps. "You're Jared's mother. I saw you at his memorial service."

Myra didn't respond.

She turned to Winston. "Her son was the Constitutional Law professor who died a few months ago. He was riding his bike… your firm is representing the driver."

"What does that have to do with anything?" He asked.

"Well, she's biracial—"

"African American," Myra interjected.

"So, then your wife is *black*? I thought you said you'd never been with a black woman before?"

Winston looked flabbergasted. "I'm afraid I don't understand…"

"Your wife has African American blood running through her veins," Myra stated. "In other words, you wasted time exploring your jungle fever. You had a black woman at home all the time." She looked over at Janet. *"You can go now."*

Winston got up and walked over to a near by window. Without turning around, he asked, "Are you and Eleanor biological sisters?"

"We had the same mom and dad—that's what you really want to know."

He turned to look at Myra, studying her. "You look…"

"But I'm not. Unlike my sister, I embrace my ethnic identity. I'm proud of who I am and I make no apologies for being born black."

"The Eleanor I've loved all these years never really existed."

"Yet, you just had your lips all over the chocolate piece that just left this room. You are no better than your ancestors. You want our goodies in the dark, but during daylight you prefer all pretty and white. But as they say, what's done in the dark will surely come to light. That includes this dirty business of yours with the D.A."

"I'm glad Eleanor has you to look after her," Winston said after a moment. "I need some time to deal with all this."

When she wasn't with Belva, Myra held a vigil at Eleanor's bedside.

"Winston was discharged today," she said. "He's gonna be fine, so don't you be worrying about him, Eleanor. Now, I need to leave for a while. Julia just texted me that the doctor is there to discuss my granddaughter's treatment."

She left the room, walking briskly to the nearest elevator, which she took to the third floor.

Julia and Vincent were in the room with Belva and the doctor.

The words chemo and radiation caught her attention. Myra's knees went weak, causing her fall.

Vincent caught her before she hit the floor. He led her over to a chair.

The doctor approached, but she waved him away. "I'll be fine. Just tell us what we need to do."

Belva reached over and took her by the hand. She was trying not to look scared, but was failing miserably.

"I'll do whatever I have to do to fight this," she told her doctor.

When he left, the family gathered around the bed as Belva began to pray.

"Father God, right now I'm caught in a whirlwind of emotions. I never thought I would get cancer. Satan wants to suck the joy right out of me and I confess that he has for the moment. I feel a bit discouraged and overwhelmed. But Father, I trust in You no matter what happens. Father, I need You to walk with me through this. Father God, I thank You for music and the peace it brings me. I will praise You in this storm, for You are who You are. Father God, I give this all to You. I trust in You and I love You."

"Amen," they said in unison.

Myra didn't touch the food Theresa brought her from the cafeteria. She didn't have an appetite. She read several passages from the Bible to calm her thoughts.

When Julia returned to the hospital later that evening, she said, "Vincent's going to stay with Belva tonight. She won't be alone."

"I'll go visit with Eleanor then."

"Mama, you're exhausted."

Myra shook her head. "Julia, I'm not gonna leave her. I don't know what Winston's planning, but I don't want Eleanor to feel abandoned."

Julia sighed in resignation.

When Vincent arrived, Belva kissed her granddaughter and said, "I'll be in Eleanor's room if you need me."

"I'm praying for her, Nana."

"Thank you, baby."

Julia walked her mother to the room where Eleanor lay. They stood side by side watching her chest rise and fall.

"Eleanor, come back to us," Myra pleaded. "*Wake up.*"

A tear slipped from her eyes. "We come from strong stock. There is nothing on this earth that we can't survive. You and I got some talking to do. Now wake up and fight."

Myra paused, watching her sister's face for a sign or something.

"Okay, well if you won't wake up, then you'll just have to lay here while I tell you the history of our family. If you don't want to hear it, then open those eyes and tell me to shut up."

Julia kissed his mother's cheek. "What time do you want me to pick you up."

Theresa had taken Myra's car back to the house. They didn't want her driving in such a high stressful condition.

"I'm gonna stay the night with her."

Julia nodded. "Okay, then I'll be back here in the morning."

"If you can bring me some clothes, I'd appreciate it."

Her daughter left just as the nurse entered the room to check Eleanor's vitals.

When she left, Myra stroked her sister's cheek. "You don't know this, but we're very lucky, Eleanor, because we're one of the few families who can trace our roots all the way to an African king in Senegal. I bet you're wondering what happened. Well, a rival tribe kidnapped his daughter when the girl was just fifteen years old and sold her into slavery. That girl's name was Ziraili…"

Chapter 5

Eleanor stared into nothingness.

That was the only way to describe it. There was no beginning, middle or end—just a neverending black hole.

The tiny hairs on the back of her neck stood up.

Eleanor felt a strong presence and thought she heard the slightest sound of something or someone moving. Fear snaked down her spine and her heart quickened.

She wasn't alone.

Terrified, she hid her face against her trembling knees afraid of the unseen, the unknown.

"Do not be afraid," a feminine voice said.

She recognized the accent as African.

Eleanor lifted her head and opened her eyes. The dark fog had lifted enough to make out the outline of a tall girl who looked to be about fifteen or so. She once again felt that same familiar, yet unfamiliar feeling. She blinked rapidly, struggling to make out more of her.

She wore torn, ragged clothing that had seen better days. Eleanor's hand fell to the crudely, stitched clothing that now covered her body, instead of the designer labels she had grown accustomed to wearing. From what she could tell, the rough fabric looked like it had been put together by hand.

"W-Who are you?" she asked in a shaky voice.

"I am Ziraili, your many-times grandmother. Beloved, I am here because I need to tell you a story—the story of your family."

"Why?" she asked.

"If you don't know your history, then you don't feel a part of it." she responded. "To move forward, you must know and understand the past."

Eleanor was too afraid to speak. She either dreaming or having a nervous breakdown. That was the only way to explain this.

"I am the daughter of a tribal King in Africa, an educated and powerful man. He was killed by another tribe and they kidnapped me during a battle. They sold me into slavery. I was placed on this ship along with hundreds of other slaves bound for America."

There was no way the woman standing before her could be her ancestor. Yet, Eleanor believed her.

She was dead. That was the other possibility.

Ziraili continued talking about her life. "I was betrayed by my own people. Tribal chiefs delivered stockades full of men and women, captured in raids and wars against other tribes. Buyers selected the finest specimens, which they bartered for weapons, ammunition, metal, liquor, trinkets, and cloth. We were loaded aboard and packed for sailing—human cargo. They chained us below decks to prevent suicides; placing us side by side to save space, row after row, one after another, until the vessel contained as many as six hundred units of human cargo."

Eleanor heard what sounded like the cry of a newborn.

She glanced around, turning in the direction of the baby's screams. Stark fear welled up in her as the edges of darkness faded away. Eleanor discovered that some how she'd been transported to a ship. The smell was repugnant to her sensitive nostrils and suffocating.

The tattered clothes on her body did not belong to her, the course fabric scratching her delicate skin. To her horror, she realized that she and Ziraili were not the only people on this ship. There were others enclosed under grated hatchways between decks. The space was so low that they sat between each other's legs, so close that lying down or changing their position was not a likely option.

She noticed on some, there were crude marks of different forms, burned into their skin. Eleanor's eyes traveled to the crying infant.

"The mother gave birth on this ship."

"What will happen to the baby?" Eleanor asked.

Ziraili did not respond.

"Why isn't she doing something? He's probably hungry."

"We are bound."

Eleanor looked down and saw the chain attached to her foot. She took in her surroundings from where she sat huddled in the corner of the slave ship. Some of the captives hung their heads down in apparently hopeless dejection; some were greatly emaciated, and some, particularly children, seemed to be dying.

Beside her a woman lay down, her eyes open but sightless in death. Her rotting flesh made Eleanor sick to her stomach.

She vomited.

For most of the human cargo, death was preferable than life.

Never had Eleanor seen such savage treatment or brutal cruelty. Hundreds packed in such close quarters, the heat of the climate, combined with the putrid smell wafting from the tubs of urine and defecation that lay below was stifling.

As the ship swayed against strong winds and the ocean waves, the groans of the dying echoed throughout the ship, across Eleanor's heart and burned in her memory. For some, it became a matter of survival with some strangling those next to them in hopes of procuring room to breathe.

A few captives took the first opportunity of leaping overboard to rid themselves of what they assumed would be an intolerable life, while others found a way to communicate, despite speaking in various dialects, and began formulating a plan to burn, blow up the ship and perish together in the flames. It seemed much better than the unknown was, and dying would be of his or her own choosing.

Ziraili glanced over at her.

"Why am I here?" Eleanor asked.

"You will soon understand."

Eleanor stared down at the chains that held her bound through watery eyes. *Please God… if you can hear me, please let me wake up from this nightmare.*

Two female captives who sought to gain favor with the crew members they were sleeping with, set out to betray the others by telling of a plan to take the ship by violence. The crew retaliated by murdering and violating the captives.

In the days that followed, an outbreak of dysentery occurred. Fearful, the crew threw the sick overboard in hopes of preventing the spreading of the illness throughout the human cargo. The captain ordered the sick killed to spare them the horror of drowning.

Eleanor stifled her scream when she saw a crew member cut off the hands and feet of a slave before throwing him overboard. She ducked her head and hid her face in her hands.

With a sorrowful heart, she continued to pray for either an end to this horrible nightmare or death. She prayed a simple, passionate prayer asking, "God have mercy upon us all."

The crew forced the slaves back down to the cramped quarters below. Panicked, Eleanor glanced around, looking for Ziraili, who silently comforted her with her gaze.

Beads of perspiration formed on Eleanor's forehead.

She moved her fingers.

Myra gasped in shock. "She just moved her fingers," she exclaimed to the nurse checking Eleanor's vitals. "That means she's waking up, don't it?"

She didn't wait for a response. Myra whispered, "I'm here, Eleanor. I'm here. Now come on back to us."

Eleanor stirred, it was slight, but Myra was encouraged. She prayed her sister was finally coming out of her coma.

Her eyelids fluttered.

"That's it. Come back to us," Myra urged. "Keep fighting. C'mon Eleanor. *Fight.*"

"Miss Myra, I don't want you to get your hopes up," the nurse stated. Keeping her voice low, she explained, "A person in a coma will sometimes make movements, sounds and they might experience agitation."

"Ziraili," Eleanor muttered in a sluggish voice.

"What did she say?" the nurse asked.

Myra frowned and shut out the noise around her, listening. She looked around the room.

Ziraili? Are you with Eleanor?

Chapter 6

September 1800

"Where are we? How did we get here?" Eleanor asked Ziraili.

One minute they were on a slave ship and now, here she was in unfamiliar surroundings, the hot sun beating down on them.

"We are on the Blanche plantation in New Orleans, Louisiana."

She glanced down at the gray-colored cotton dress she was wearing. Eleanor put a trembling hand to her head, which was covered in plaits. She felt like herself, but she wasn't herself—her skin was no longer a tawny color. She was a smooth, tortoise shell brown with black tightly coiled hair.

"Come," she said. "You'll understand everything very soon."

Eleanor surveyed her surroundings as she walked with Ziraili.

One-room log cabins, some whitewashed on the outside lined up in a crude row. The buildings were windowless, some with wooden shutters while others had makeshift curtains. Beside each house was a little plot of yard for gardens to raise vegetables.

A couple of chickens crossed her path, running from the children chasing them.

A passing slave woman greeted Ziraili, and then said, "Nellie, you is certainly growing like a weed, chile."

Confused, Eleanor glanced up at Ziraili. "Nellie? Why did she call me that?"

"You have the honor of living in the body of my daughter. She is Nellie." She led her into a cabin where she picked up a broken piece of a mirror.

A young girl who looked around thirteen stared back at Eleanor. "This isn't me."

"You are Nellie. This is her life."

"I don't understand."

"To understand your future, you need to know the past." Ziraili led her into what Eleanor considered a wooden shack, saying. "This is our home."

She stared at the rudimentary hearth used for cooking, and probably for heating water for bathing, drinking—whatever. Her mouth dropped open at the sight of dirt floors.

Ziraili greeted her man with a kiss. She paused her sweeping and stroked his cheek. Turning to Eleanor, she said, "The missus wants us to git that dress finished quick like. Now c'mon. We got to get over to Old Mastah's house."

She wiped her hands in the folds of her dress. "August, I made some cracklin' bread, collards and there's a little piece of hen left. I'll be back as soon as Missus is done wit us."

She fussed the whole time they walked up the road to the big house.

As they neared the house, Ziraili placed an arm around Nellie and said, "I want you to stay right under me, you hear me chile. That Mastah Andre been eyeing you hard lately. You got to be careful 'round him, gal. He'll have you with your skirts over your head in no time."

Eleanor nodded. She was too afraid to say anything.

"Nellie, who you bobbing your head at? Cat suddenly got your tongue?"

"No ma'am," she responded.

"We got to git over to the house. C'mon chile."

"Ziraili, there you are," Missus stated as soon as they entered through the back door. "It's about time."

Her mother took her by the hand and rushed to a room off the side of the house where yards of fabric were stacked on a table.

As instructed, Nellie sat beside her mother and picked up a needle.

"I want you to finish the hem on this dress," her mother directed. She picked up a shimmery piece of taffeta. "I have to finish sewing on that piece of lace Missus wants around the neckline of this dress."

Nellie rubbed her calloused hands together, and then went to her sewing. The Missus would be hopping mad. She had been helping her mother with the sewing since she was big enough to thread a needle.

"We raise de wheat, dey gib us de corn; we bake de bread…" Nellie heard one of the men singing as he headed out to the cotton field. She soon found herself humming along as she worked.

She dropped her head when the Missus swept into the room in an emerald green dress with a white satin ribbon around the bodice that contrasted with the simple gray cotton dresses Nellie and her mother wore. The slaves could never look their owners straight in the face. It was a sign of disrespect.

Ann Blanche ignored Nellie, speaking directly to her mother. "I declare Ziraili, you do such good work. Do be sure to have that dress ready for me by tomorrow morning. I want to wear it when my parents come for supper."

"Yes ma'am," she responded. "I'll have it right and ready."

"Nellie, now you hand me that thread over there. I got to hurry up and finish wit this one fore I finish Missus dress. She gon' be wantin' this blue one today."

"Yes ma'am," Nellie whispered.

As she worked, her eyes traveled over to the

dress hanging in the corner. The fancy gown was adorned with clasps, puffy sleeves and high waist. Nellie knew that she would never be able to wear something so grand. The fabric was silky and smooth while she and the other slaves were forced to wear clothes made from a scratchy coarse material.

Her mother along with two other women did the sewing for everyone on the plantation. Nellie was being trained by her mother to be a seamstress.

The other two women lived outside the room where they worked. They slept in the passage on mats that rolled up during the day. The missus favored Ziraili so she could go home to her family at the end of the workday.

Theodore Blanche, called Old Mastah by his slaves was a quiet, soft-spoken man who owned a medium-sized plantation and was reputed a kind owner when it came to his slaves. Unlike some slave owners, he gave them Saturday afternoon, all day Sunday off, half a day on Thanksgiving and Christmas. He and his wife were kind toward the slaves. They had two sons, Andre and Herbert.

When they weren't working for Old Mastah, the slaves spent their time off washing clothes, cleaning their cabins and tending their gardens. Saturday nights were often of singing and dancing while Sundays were reserved for religious teaching which Old Mastah provided. Slaves often went fishing, hunting or visiting other plantations in the afternoons.

Despite the kindness of their owner, there were those who yearned for freedom. Whispers of it traveled through the slave grapevine, embedded in songs and even stitched in quilts.

Nellie's father was one of the slaves who had such dreams. She had heard him mention it a time or two whenever her parents thought she was asleep.

One night, Nellie thought she heard screams riding on the wind. She wrapped a shawl around her arms to ward off the chill she felt.

She could hear the low murmurs dancing back and forth between her parents.

Nellie heard her mother crying as her father left. They had been arguing about something, but she couldn't hear what it was about. Still, a cloud of uneasiness settled within her.

It stayed with Nellie the next day, and the day after that.

Her mother was bothered by something as well—Nellie could see it all over her face, although she made attempts to put on a brave front for her and her siblings.

A few nights later, Nellie caught sight of her father leaving the house when he eased past her window.

Determined to find out what was going on, Nellie got up out of the straw-stuffed bed she shared with her two older siblings and followed her father, holding the ends her shawls together.

Between two cabins, groups of men gathered around a small oil lamp. There were men posted on opposite ends of the slave quarters.

They were lookouts, Nellie assumed.

August must have felt as if someone watched from the shadows. His head spun from side to side, his eyes swiftly searching the area.

They landed on her.

Nellie met his gaze for a moment before disappearing between the cabins. She ran back into their house and eased back into bed, praying that he wouldn't mention this to her mother.

Ziraili didn't box her ears the next day, so Nellie assumed her father kept their little secret.

"You know Marse Andre can't keep his eyes offa you," one of the girls teased Nellie. "I hear tell he gon' be visiting you soon."

Nellie shook her head as she helped her friend take down the laundry from the clothes line behind the big house. "I don't like the way he be lookin' at me."

"Here he come now," Sissy whispered.

Both girls concentrated on their work.

He eyed them for a moment, a smile on his lips, and then rode off on his horse.

Later that evening, August woke up Nellie after everyone else was asleep.

She sat up in bed. "Daddy, is something wrong?"

"Nellie, I want you to pray to God… pray to Him when you happy and pray to Him when you sad."

There was something in her father's voice—a sense of urgency that made Nellie listen intently, trying to memorize his every word.

Before she could respond to her father, he walked purposefully towards the door. Her mother got up and tried to stop him from leaving, but she couldn't compete with August's willful determination.

Ziraili fell to her knees, praying fervently, with tears running down her face.

A few hours later, loud screams awakened Nellie. She whispered a prayer for her father. "God, please give my father his freedom."

She heard gunshots.

They killed my daddy.

Sobs rip through her throat and tore pass her lips.

Ziraili rushed over, clamping her mouth over Nellie's mouth to drown out her cries while holding her tight. Her own tears mingled with those of her daughter. The other children held onto them, burying their tears in their mother's dress.

Wiping her face, she whispered, "Hush y'all. Your father is free now. Thank the Lawd that he free… no more sufferings of this here world. He free… my heart is sad but the Lawd gon' give me strength to go on." She kissed each of them. "Go back to sleep. Morning be here soon."

Fourteen-year-old Nellie sat on her little porch darning a sheet and enjoying the warmth of the sun. She kept her needle moving as she watched the children playing outside.

Her next-door neighbor walked over and sat down beside her. "I hear Mattie been messing 'round wit dat boy dat come from Georgia, and now she carryin; a bun in the oven."

Nellie glanced over at the gossipy Sooky and said. "Ain't they getting married?"

"If Old Mastah say so." She rose to her feet. "When I was livin' on de Willis Plantation, us lived in a one room log cabin, but it was a big room and had a plank floor and a big fireplace dat kept us plenty warm in de wintertime. De beds was nailed to de wall. We sho' had it good dere. Us had slats on our beds."

"Sounds like you was livin' it up in Georgia," Nellie stated. "If you lucky, you get to sleep on a straw bed or a mat here." She liked Sooky well enough, but the girl was always talking about what she had on that plantation in Georgia. Sooky had been on Blanche Plantation going on six months.

"I was a house-girl before coming here," Sooky stated. "I did de ironing and a heap of house work. Us house women et at de table in de kitchen. Us had jest as good eating as de white folks."

"Why they sell you?" Nellie asked.

Elsie frowned. "De Mistis was jealous of me and Massa Jeff. He used to come to me for comfort. I had my own cabin jest like you." She grinned. "You must be comforting Massa Andre right fine. I see him leaving de cabin 'most every night."

Nellie felt her cheeks go warm. She concentrated on her sewing.

She hated every moment she spent with Massa Andre. He had forced himself on her the week after her father had been gunned down trying to escape. Her mother had begged with him to leave Nellie alone, but her pleas were ignored.

She shifted her position in the chair, trying to get comfortable. The baby in her belly moved.

"Dey used to tan leather out of cow hides and make shoes for us to wear in de wintertime," Sooky stated. "I tell you da truth. Dem shoes sho was rough and hard, but dey kept your feet dry and warm."

"Old Mastah make sure we have shoes to wear," Nellie responded. "That the one thing he do."

"Mistis tried to learn us to read," Sooky-bragged. "I never did learn much. I sho' miss my man." A flash of sadness crossed her face. "I jumped de broom wit Tom. He worked on a neighboring plantation. Us had two babies when dey sold me. I pray you be able to hold onto de chile growing in your belly."

"Massa Andre had Old Mastah sell off my brothers Jacob and Samuel. It's just me, Mama and Benjamin left here."

"Your brother is a fine-looking buck," Sooky stated. "He got a woman?"

Nellie gave her friend a sidelong glance. "I knew you was eyeing him. His woman was sold last year. Benjamin grieved her for a long time."

Nellie placed a protective hand on her stomach just as Leal appeared from around the corner.

She had been in love with him from the time she was twelve years old. Nellie knew that Leal loved her, too.

He knew that the child she carried belonged to their owner's son. Massa Andre ordered Leal to stay out of Nellie's bed until after she delivered his child.

Sooky babbled on and on about her former life in Georgia while Nellie watched Leal chopping wood for the old midwife, they called Big Sis. When her time came, Big Sis would bring her child into the world.

It won't be long now, she thought silently.

Later that night under the shadows of darkness, Nellie suffered through the throes of hard labor.

She heard Leal's voice and turned in that direction. He was standing in the doorway, a look of concern on his face.

He came closer to the bed and stroked her cheek. "I'll always love you," he said in a low voice before leaving the room.

Nellie cried out for Leal as she struggled to bring forth her child into the world. She labored for almost ten hours before giving birth to a daughter.

She took one look at the child and burst into loud sobs. "She a white child…"

"Hush now, that babe came from yo body. She yo chile."

"I don't want no white baby," Nellie uttered.

Big Sis leaned over her and said, "Gal, you better bury that thought away, cause this lil' gal gone need you."

A hush fell over the room when Andre Blanche entered the slave quarters to see the new addition along with his new bride, who paled at the sight of the light-skinned infant. She left quickly.

"She's a beauty," he murmured. "I'm gonna name her Sybil."

"That's a fine name," Big Sis said.

Nellie refused to look at him or the infant.

A couple of months later, Nellie and Leal married, bringing great joy back into her life. However, it wasn't until Andre's wife got pregnant that he left Nellie alone for good.

Two years and a couple of miscarriages later, she gave birth to another daughter—this one fathered by Leal.

Chapter 7

Andre's wife could no longer bear the sight of Sybil because she strongly resembled her husband, so she sold Nellie and her daughters, a week after he died to her cousin in Savannah, Georgia. Leal had dropped dead out in a field just weeks before Andre's death. Before she left, her mother came to her saying, "No matter where you go, I will be with you. We share the same heartbeat as those of our ancestors. They can sell us, but our hearts will always find a way to connect."

Nellie cried no tears as the wagon pulled away. Her sorrow was so deep that it was be-

80

yond tears. Her grief did not last long, however.

Nellie met and fell in love with Luke, when she was a newcomer on the Gerard plantation in 1820. They decided to ask for permission to marry after she discovered she was pregnant. Their son, James was born three months after their wedding. They had another son the following year.

One day she walked into the shack to find her husband in deep thought and asked, "Luke, what you thinking so hard on?"

"Some of the slaves been talking," he began. "There's talk of slaves takin' a railroad to freedom up north."

Remembering the way her father had died, Nellie gave him a look of disbelief. "That's foolish talk. I don't know about this, Luke. It just don't sound right." Scanning his face, she added, "Don't you go thinkin' crazy. We got four children here that needs you."

"I want sumpthin' better for us, Nellie. If there is a way to get it—I have to try."

She folded her arms across her chest. "So, it don't matter what I say, huh?"

Luke kissed her. "I love you, gal, but there are a group of slaves heading out tonight. I got to go wit them."

"What if you get caught? What then? My daddy was shot dead for trying to escape."

"We ain't gon' think like that."

Nellie wiped away her tears. "If you mean to do this fool thing, then you best go with God."

She moved about the room, packing a knapsack of dried meats and cornbread for Luke and praying for his safe return one day.

Shortly after midnight, Nellie kissed her husband goodbye.

She fell to her knees and stayed there for over an hour, just talking to God and asking Him to spare Luke's life. She was scared for him because Nellie knew what happened to runaway slaves if they were caught by slave hunters.

Just as she said, "Amen," the door opened and to her surprise, Luke was standing there, a strange look in his gaze.

Nellie threw herself into his arms. "Luke, what happened? What made you come back? Did you change your mind?"

Luke quickly blew out the candles to make the cabin dark, and pulled Nellie over to the pallet where they slept.

A shiver ran down Nellie's spine. "What happened?" she asked a second time.

He was shaking so hard, that he could barely get the words out. Nellie wrapped her arms around him. A tear rolled down his cheek.

Nellie held her breath for what was to come.

"I was headed out to join Neb, Jimmy and Lett. That's when I heard the horses. Nellie, it sounded like a hunnard of them."

"What happened to Neb and them?" she asked as calmly as she could manage.

"I saw they white faces. It was 'bout six or seven of them buckras surrounding Neb and Jimmy. Some of the riders caught Lett and drug him back to where the others were." Luke took a deep breath, then released it. "They tortured my friends and there was nothing I could do."

"Are they…"

He nodded. "They shot them dead. Nellie, if you hadn't kept me here… I'd be right there with them—dead. You saved my life, baby."

Nellie wrapped her arms around him. "Thank you, God," she whispered. "Thank you for bringing my man back to me."

Outside, they heard horses in the distance.

Luke held onto Nellie as if his life depended on it.

She felt the hair on the back of her neck stand up. She couldn't dismiss the sensation that they were being watched and a thread of fear coursed through her.

Had Luke been seen?

She stole a glance over her shoulder and gasped. Nellie rushed to her feet and ran toward the window.

Luke followed her. "What is it, Nellie? Did you see someone?"

She nodded.

He looked scared. "Was it one of them buckras looking in here?"

Nellie shook her head no. "It was Ziraili. My mama."

Luke was confused. "How can that be? You got word that she died three months ago."

"I can't explain it, but I tell you true, it was my mama. Seeing her on a night like this is a sign that we gon' be fine. Now let's go to bed and try to get some sleep. Morning gonna be upon us before we know it."

***

Belva was out of the hospital and ready to have her first round of chemo.

Myra picked up one of the brochures on Leukemia lying on the table beside her. We can't fight it if we don't understand the way it works, she thought to herself. Her faith was strong. Belva was going to come out of this completely healed. She believed it.

Her thoughts turned to Eleanor. She had been in a coma for a week now, and hadn't moved much or made a sound since that last time.

Myra closed her eyes and began to pray, asking God to give her granddaughter the strength to fight off this horrible disease and for Eleanor to wake up.

"Father God, I forgive my sister. I do. I don't understand why she made the choices she made, but I forgive her. Just please give me the chance to tell her."

When her treatment was completed, Vincent escorted Belva to the car.

Myra stood up. "How'd she do?"

"Just fine," he responded. "I'm going to take her home so she can rest."

"I didn't sleep well last night," Belva said.

"I kept thinking about today. Nana, how is Eleanor?"

"The same."

"I'm praying for her."

"Thank you, baby," Myra said. "I'll give you a call later on."

Belva hugged her. "I love you, Nana."

"I love you, too."

She went to Eleanor's room.

"Mrs. Madison," one of her church members walked over to her. "I heard some of the nurses saying that you and Eleanor Blakemore are sisters. Is that true?"

"Rachel, it's true," Myra responded.

"I also heard that her husband hasn't been here since he was discharged."

"He was also in the car," Myra responded. "I think it's best for him to build up his strength right now. I assured him that I would look after Eleanor."

"Bless your heart. You are always looking out for others. How's Belva doing?"

"She's just fine." Myra wasn't going to share her granddaughter's business with the nurse. It was Belva's choice if she wanted people to know."

"Well, I need to get to my sister."

"I'll be in there shortly to check her vitals."

Myra rolled her eyes heavenward as she strolled into the room. Rachel was a gossip. This business with Eleanor was going to be all over town. It didn't bother her much because Myra didn't care about people knowing the truth.

Eleanor might feel different, but there wasn't anything Myra could do to change it. Getting her sister to open her eyes was more important to her than idle gossip.

Eleanor was back in a dark void.

She gasped, realizing a shiver of panic.

"Ziraili," she whispered, frantically searching out the nothingness. "Where are you? Please don't leave me." She couldn't breathe and panted in terror. Eleanor hated the total darkness and experienced disturbing quakes in her serenity.

"Beloved, you are not alone," Ziraili responded.

She couldn't see her, but Eleanor felt the warmth of her presence.

"Where are we?"

The fog dissipated slowly.

"You are still on the Gerard Plantation, only now you will inhabit the body of my grand-daughter, Sybil."

"Nellie's oldest daughter with Andre Blanche," she said. Eleanor rubbed her arms to ward off the chill of the cool weather, noting the tawny color of her skin.

Ziraili nodded.

Sybil had fair skin and straight, dark hair that reached her waist. She could have easily passed for white. At the time of her birth, her father was one of the wealthiest planta-tion owners in New Orleans. After Sybil was weaned, she was taken from Nellie and raised in the household of her white grandmother and father, despite the protests of his wife.

After Andre's death, his widow sold her along with her mother and sister. However, Sybil was returned to the Gerard Plantation at the request of Andre's brother upon his sister-in-law's death. He paid a large sum for Sybil's return to honor his dying mother's request that the girl remain with family.

Although she was back on the plantation

where she was born, Sybil displayed no emotion one way or the other. Regardless of being fathered by a Gerard, she knew her place and it wasn't in the warm arms of family.

"Sybil, I declare you are the quietest slave we have," Elizabeth Gerard told her as she prepared a powder used to cure headaches. "I greatly appreciate your ability to not prattle on and on especially when I'm having one of my spells."

"Yes ma'am," Sybil responded. She held out the glass to her mistress who nearly gulped it down. She had been working with a slave called Nan, who knew how to mix herbs and other healing powders.

"Close the curtains, Sybil. My eyes are extremely sensitive to the light."

She did as she was told and left the room.

Sybil made her way downstairs.

Her owners were loved by most of their slaves, except a few like Sybil, who were embittered by the separation of families.

There were days that Sybil wished they would all just drop dead.

.

Chapter 8

By midsummer 1838, an outbreak of yellow fever had ravaged cities all along the Mississippi River. According to the slave grapevine, the *fever* spread from the docks and crept toward the plantations, threatening everyone but the slaves. The Gerard's had family in Virginia, but there was no use in traveling there because they were also losing victims to the disease at an alarming rate.

The cemeteries in the city were filling with fever victims, turning fear to panic and causing thousands to flee the city.

The fever soon made its way to the Gerard

Plantation.

Sybil ran herself weary trying to care for the sick. Old man Gerard was the first one stricken. He was dead before anyone realized what had happened.

The mistress of the house had a time on her hand consoling her grief-stricken husband over the death of his father.

"Missus, why don't you lay down for a spell?" Sybil suggested one day when the woman looked as if she were about to collapse from exhaustion. "You plumb tired."

"I fear my husband..." she couldn't even finish the sentence. "He loved his father dearly."

"Yes ma'am." Sybil had no feelings for her master. He was a harsh man when it came to his slaves, but his wife had no tolerance for cruelty. He'd had one woman whipped because she stole a ham. When the Missus found out, she took to her bed for a week and according to slave gossip, locked him out of her bedroom.

Sybil encouraged her mistress to rest her body once more. This time the woman agreed.

"I'm going to lay down for a spell," she said. "Please come get me if Mr. Gerard requires my presence. Oh, take Abby down to the kitchen. I told Etta to make her something to eat."

Her head bowed, Sybil replied, "Yes ma'am, Missus. I'll come get you."

She went to Abby's room.

"Abby, chile, I needs to take you downstairs for some good food."

"My head hurts," the small child complained.

"That's 'cause you hungry."

She smiled. "I hope Etta has biscuits and honey."

"I just bet she does. Just for you, Abby girl."

Hand in hand, they made their way downstairs. Sybil noted that her skin was just as light as Abby's. If she were dressed in her mistress's finery—no one would know that she was a slave. They would never be able to tell.

She delivered Abby to Etta, who told her that a couple of slaves in their quarters had fallen sick.

Worried sick by the news, Sybil found a quiet corner in the house to pray. *"Lord, we need you to show up right now. We beg of you to send your angels to keep charge over this here plantation. Protect us from the fever that is kill-*

ing folks around here. We need you Lord. We need you. Amen."

As the fever spread, there were rumors of husbands abandoning wives and family. Sybil spent her days at the big house caring for the sick. While many plantation owners died, or left the city, the slaves stayed on to minister to the sick.

Sybil's countenance faltered the very moment the missus' daughter complained of a headache and began vomiting.

"Missus," she screamed as she ran through the house. "Abby is sick, Missus."

The woman paled. "Is it the fever?"

Sybil responded, "I think so, ma'am. Her little body is hot as fire."

The missus had Sybil put the child to bed and stay with her around the clock. She and one of the other slaves did everything they could to save the child, including prayer, but despite their efforts, the child died a few days later.

Sybil understood what it felt like to lose a child as her oldest daughter lived only six years and her son Josiah was sold when he was only five years old shortly after she gave birth to her third child Sam.

Her mistress, despondent over the death of her only child, refused to leave her bed after the funeral, willing herself to die.

"Missus, I brought you something to eat," Sybil announced as she entered the bedroom.

Her mistress groaned, and then turned away.

"Marse Gerard is fitfully worried about you, Missus. He just lost his father and little Abby. He don't want to lose you."

After a few days, her mistress seemed to be getting better.

"Missus, I brought you something to eat," Sybil announced as she entered the bedroom.

She was surprised to find the woman up and about. One of the other slaves was in the room helping her dress.

"Missus, you're bright as sunshine today," Sybil told her when the other girl left the room. "Praise the Lord."

She smiled. "Sybil, I don't think I could've made it without you taking such good care of me. I want you to know that I now understand how you must have felt when you lost your children."

"It was painfully hard," Sybil admitted as

she sat the tray laden with food down on a nearby table.

"I give you my word that Sam will never be taken from you. I will never allow him to be sold. I already told this to Mr. Gerard and he agrees with me."

"Thank you, Missus. Thank you."

"Mr. Gerard informed me that we could get almost two hundred dollars for Sam, but because of your loyalty and the way you took care of his father and Abby... and me, he desired to reward you." She sat down at the table and lifted the silver cover. "Everything smells delicious."

Her cell phone rang, waking Myra.

"Hello," she murmured.

"Mama, it's Julia. I just wanted to check on Eleanor. Has there been any change?"

"No, I'm afraid not."

"I talked to Mike. With everything that's going on now with Belva—I should be there with her. I'll be driving in this evening. I hope you don't mind my staying at the house."

"Honey, that's your home. Of course I don't mind. Besides, I've been spending most of my time here at the hospital."

"Belva told me that you're always there with her when she has her treatments. I think you're spreading yourself too thin, Mama. Once I get there, I'll look after Belva and you focus on your sister."

"We'll talk about it when you come, Julia. Now you be safe on the road, sugar. I don't want nothing happening to you."

"The Lord's going to be with me."

"Amen," Myra said with a smile. "There's food in the refrigerator and your old room has clean linen. I changed it yesterday while I was at the house."

"I'll see you this evening, Mama."

"Okay baby. God be with you."

Myra rose to her feet slowly. Some days her knees worked with her and then other days, she could barely stand.

Today's a good day, she thought when joints didn't protest.

She was glad that Julia was coming home. Lord knows, she was trying to be in two places at the same time. Myra couldn't abandon Belva or Eleanor.

Her gaze traveled to the woman she'd been so angry with since finding out she was still alive.

A thought occurred to her.

What would happen when Eleanor finally came out of the coma?

Cold weather finally ended the yellow fever outbreak, in late October.

Having gained the favor of her mistress, Sybil became her confidante. She was the first one that the woman told when she discovered she was pregnant.

Sybil moved into the house to care for her mistress while she was bedridden for the remainder of her pregnancy after a fall.

Mastah Gerard was away often during this time. Sybil knew that he had been frequenting the slave quarters, but would never tell her mistress. When Becca delivered her baby in three or four months, the Missus would discover the truth for herself.

Sybil liked her mistress enough, but she still

held onto her anger from the sale of her son Josiah. She grieved him as much as she grieved for Molly Ann, her firstborn. She didn't want to lose Sam, too.

However, Mastah Gerard had a change of heart after his wife died during a difficult childbirth. Blaming Sybil for his wife's death, he sold ten-year-old Sam that same year to a slave owner in Maryland.

Sybil had to be physically restrained to keep from trying to attack Mastah Gerard. It broke her heart to hear her son crying out for her. She could see the fear in his eyes.

She hated the world they lived in. Families were ripped apart at will and there was nothing they could do about it.

What kind of God allowed this?

In her heart, she knew the answer. He was the same one who had freed his children all those years before. Sybil knew she had to put her faith in the God of Abraham and of Moses.

Angry, Sybil wrapped the Missus's old Bible in a piece of calico fabric and gave it to her son. She made Sam promise to keep it with him always.

Sybil didn't feel guilty for stealing the Bible.

She felt betrayed after the many years of loyal service she provided to the Gerard family.

She and a group of other slaves talked in the shadows of darkness the night after Sam was ripped from her arms.

"I'm leaving," Sybil blurted. "I can't stay here anymore."

"What you gon' do?" one of the men asked. "You gon' try to run away?"

She gave him a hard stare. "What *you* gonna do?"

"Tomorrow night," he muttered. "After the stroke of midnight, I'll be under that there oak tree near the road."

Another man nodded in agreement.

The two men peeked out before leaving her cabin.

Sybil blew out all but one candle.

She moved stealthily around the room, packing up enough food to last for several days.

When time came, Sybil met the men she'd be traveling with as planned. She pulled out a sack of cayenne pepper and picked up a limb full of leaves, using it to erase their footprints. She sprinkled the cayenne pepper to throw off the dogs.

They walked away from the road, hidden in the brushes.

When the sun rose, they found an abandoned barn and after covering themselves with straw, sought sleep.

Sybil was awakened hours later by the sound of horses outside. She was too afraid to move a muscle.

Ira, the man beside her, whispered. "Don't move. Just stay still."

They heard the door open, and someone below said, "Ain't no niggers in here. The dogs can't pick up no scent. They long gone from here."

Sybil's heart raced and thumped so loudly that she feared the slave catchers below could hear it.

They heard the man walk out the door, but Sybil and the men were too afraid to move. Sometimes, the slave catchers pretended to leave and slaves caught. Ira had attempted to run away in the past, but was beaten and returned to the plantation.

Sybil heard the riders leaving, but still they did not move. Someone could have stayed behind.

She had no idea how long they just lay there.

Ira sat up first, brushing the straw off his body. He cautioned them to stay put while he went to check out their surroundings.

"If I'm not back by nightfall, don't wait for me and don't stay here. Dey might come back just to make sure no slaves hiding out."

Sybil glanced over at Jacob, her other traveling partner and nodded.

It was almost dark when Ira returned. She and Jacob were on their way out of the barn when they heard his whistle.

Luck would not carry them far.

Ira must have been spotted at some point and the slave catchers followed him back to the barn.

Sybil took off running when she heard the white riders coming towards them. Prickly bushes tore at her skirt, but she didn't care. She wanted to get away.

Ira and Jacob kept yelling for her not to look back. They told her to keep running.

She fell, got up and took off running again.

She could hear one of the riders getting closer and closer.

Sybil ran as fast as she could, but tripped over a fallen tree branch, twisting her ankle in the process.

The man got off his horse and began walking toward her, the look on his face menacing.

Sybil screamed…

Chapter 9

"My great-grandson Sam never knew what happened to his mother after he left the Gerard plantation," Ziraili explained to Eleanor.

She could only hear her voice as they were back in that dreadful sea of blackness. "Do you know what happened to him?" Eleanor asked.

She did not respond.

"Sam... what happened to him?"

"As he grew up, he watched his master closely, recognizing that he was an evil sort of man, very hard and rash," Ziraili stated. "When Sam was 16, he was sold again, this time to a man named Ben Taylor. Upon his arrival on the

Taylor Plantation, he fell in love with a slave named Linah the following year. He had three daughters, Ruth Anne, Isabel, and Sophie. Three women who shaped their own destiny."

"I don't understand..." Eleanor said, but then she realized that she no longer felt Ziraili presence.

She was all alone.

May 1856

Ruth Anne was in the throes of a nightmare.

The night heat felt stifling and the slight breeze through the window did nothing to cool her restless body. Sweat poured from her forehead onto the makeshift feather pillow.

Ruth Anne held onto the Bible her father had given her the night before she married George Jackson, close to her chest.

"P-Please don't..." she mumbled. No more..." Ruth Anne's head swayed back and forth as she struggled in her sleep. She continued talking sometimes the words came out clear and other times incoherently.

A faceless man kissed Ruth Anne on her mouth as she groped he body, and tried to force her legs open.

She bolted upward in bed, yelling, "NOOO!"

Terrified, Ruth Ann surveyed her surroundings.

Her racing heart gradually returned to normal as Ruth Anne realized that she was alone in her own bed.

It was just a dream.

A little boy got up and scrambled over to the bed.

Ruth Anne smiled as she pulled her youngest son Joshua close to her. She awarded him a kiss.

He placed his ear on her stomach. In his excitement at movement of the baby, Joshua knocked over the water jar sitting on a stand next to the bed.

George came running into the room. When he saw that she was not in danger, he stood in the doorway, just staring at her, his expression blank and watched as Ruth Anne tried to reach for the wet rag lying on the floor.

"George, can you help me please?" she pleaded. "For goodness sake, where is Isabel? Did she leave already?"

At that moment, a woman entered the house and pushed past George. She picked up the jar and cleaned up the floor. "I's right here, Ruth Anne. I was 'bout to get some collards out the garden and cook them for supper."

She found a clean rag to wipe the sweat from her sister's forehead. Mastah Joe assigned Isabel to take care of her, because this pregnancy was not going as well as the others.

Ruth Anne had been healthy as a horse with Joshua, but this one—she was sick and weak through most of the pregnancy and now confined to her bed until she gave birth.

Ruth Anne's mood veered from happiness to a deep sadness as she avoided looking into the eyes of her husband. A wave of guilt washed over her as she knew deep down, she was the cause of his angst and suspicions that the child she carried may have been fathered by Mastah Joe.

Isabel glanced over at George, staring him down. She was a year younger than Ruth Anne, but very little scared her. She had an ugly-looking scar on her back because of the severe beating she received after trying to kill the overseer when he tried to rape her.

A few days after the beating, the overseer doubled over in pain and died before anyone could get to him. The owners believing some type of voodoo was involved, became fearful of Isabel. The mistress no longer wanted her to help prepare meals, so she was told to care for her sister and other pregnant slaves.

Ruth Anne found her sister's touch strong yet loving and gentle. She knew Isabel had heard the rumors, but they didn't faze her. She took pleasure in her owner's fear.

Isabel gave George an admonishing look that sent him out of the cabin so that the two women could be alone.

"Thank you," Ruth Anne whispered.

"If he ain't helpin,' then he don't need to be standin' 'round here in the way. I heard you screaming. You had that same dream again?"

Ruth Anne nodded. "I can't bear the hurt I see in George's eyes. When I wake up from these dreams, he knows what it's about. But what bothers me is the thirst for revenge that I know George is carrying 'round." She appreciated that her sister wasn't like some of the women who liked to engage in slave gossip.

Ruth Anne worried what George would do if her child belonged to Mastah Joe. He was a jealous man with a violent temper at times. She had caught him a few times eyeing the Mastah, the look of cold fury in his dark eyes. She didn't blame him for feeling the way he did, but Ruth Ann feared that he would soon act on that anger.

They were owned by a white slave master and considered property. Their master could do as he pleased, which included taking liberties with her, and George was helpless to prevent it.

Her husband admitted to having mixed feelings about the child she carried. If it were his seed—he vowed to love and protect as a father should, but if the child was their master's issue…

Ruth Anne and George argued constantly about this situation. She loved her child no matter who fathered it, and she wanted her husband to accept the baby. Mastah Joe would never recognize the child and if his wife was offended by the sight of the child—he or she would be sold to another owner.

George was a man with a hot temper. Mastah Joe often called him a rebellious slave. He had tried for years to break him, and finally succeeded when their owner violated George's beloved Ruth Ann.

"This don't feel right," Ruth Anne said when she felt a sharp pain stab her. "I got a terrible feeling that something's wrong."

She groaned when another pain hit her.

Isabel placed both hands to Ruth Anne's face. "Just try to relax. Stop your worrying about George 'cause everything is gon' be fine between y'all. Just trust in the good Lord above."

"I don't know what I'd do without you, Isabel," Ruth Anne stated with a small smile as she placed a protective arm around her belly.

Isabel stole a peek out the window, then turned back to face Ruth Anne, saying, "The children have been fed and bathed. George is gone. I think he went fishing with some of the other men."

"Check the door," Ruth Anne instructed. She didn't want them getting interrupted or worse, caught by Mastah Raymond or that nosy overseer he hired two weeks ago.

Isabel did as she was told, then returned to her sister's bedside, saying, "I closed it good."

Ruth Anne lifted the sheet, pulled out the Bible, and read to Isabel. She didn't read as she normally did, because Ruth Anne felt tired. The more her pregnancy progressed, the weaker she grew.

"I love hearing this part where Moses leads the Israelites out of slavery," Isabel stated, a big smile on her face. There were rumors traveling down the slave grapevine that she was going to be sold to an owner in the South.

"I know what you're planning," Ruth Ann said. She knew Isabel had no intentions of letting that happen.

Isabel gazed at her sister. "I'm not going down South. I heard they terrible mean to they slaves. There won't be another man to lay his whip to my back again. *And live to tell it.*"

"You know what happens to slaves when they get caught."

"I ain't getting caught, Ruth Anne. I'll die before I let them catch me."

"How can you be so sure? So many slaves have tried to escape. Remember Uncle Jet? They chopped off his foot."

"Ziraili came to me in a dream last night. She told me to leave the night you give birth to this baby. That's what I'm gon' do."

"I don't want Sophie and my babies to stay in slavery. You got to get them out. Promise me."

"I will. I promise Ruth Anne."

Isabel picked up the rag and wiped her sister's brow. "Close your eye and rest."

Humming softly, she sat there watching over Ruth Anne as she fell asleep.

When Isabel left Ruth Anne's cabin, a young light-skinned woman was waiting outside for her.

Her eyes darted around, searching for a moment before she said, "I tell you true… dey gon' sell you, Isabel. Now dis man—he came taday, and he slipped dis to me and say gib to you."

She took the paper, hugged the woman and thanked her. "Go back to the big house before you get caught by the overseer."

After the woman left, Isabel went into the

cabin she shared with her sister Sophie.

It was time to execute her plan, Isabel thought as she stared down at the piece of paper with two names written on it.

The next day while bathing Ruth Anne with a damp cloth, she began to sing *Amazing Grace.*

"Amazing grace, how sweet the sound, that saved a wretch like me.... I once was lost but now am found, was blind, but now, I see... T'was grace that taught... my heart to fear. And grace, my fears relieved. How precious did that grace appear... the hour I first believed. Through many dangers, toils and snares... we have already come. T'was grace that brought us safe thus far... and grace will lead us home ..."

She kept repeating the last sentence. "... *And grace will lead me home, grace will lead me home.*"

Ruth Anne's eyes filled with tears as she comprehended what this meant for her sister.

She gave Isabel an approving nod and said in a whispering voice, "May God be with you from now to freedom."

They were careful to keep their voices down in a low voice as Isabel shared her plan with the one person she knew she could trust.

Ruth Anne groaned and shifted her position in bed.

"You still having those pains?" Isabel inquired.

She nodded.

"All that worrying ain't good for you or that baby," Isabel stated. "It's important to stay calm."

"I just wish the pain would stop," Ruth Anne said. "I didn't go through this when I was carrying my other children."

By nightfall, Ruth Anne's condition was getting worse, and she was experiencing severe contractions, so George had Isabel summoned to the cabin.

Ruth Anne was still in pain, only this time, the contractions did not wane as they had in the past.

"I think the baby's coming," George said when Isabel arrived.

"I'll go inside and see what is going on," she stated. When she made it through the door, she laid eyes on that ol' hateful Mastah Joe.

Isabel dropped her eyes and waited for him to pass.

"She's in great pain," He told her. "That baby is coming soon. Have someone alert me when the child is born."

"Yessum," she responded.

George sat outside the cabin with a scowl plastered on his face. Isabel sent him a warning glance before entering the cabin.

Ruth Anne was groaning in agony.

Isabel picked up a wet washcloth and gently wiped the sweat off her forehead. "I's right here, sister."

There was more moaning and clawing at the sheets as she writhed in pain.

Ruth Anne gathered the strength to pull Isabel closer. "Go," she whispered. "You need to leave here."

"I want to make sure you and that baby okay."

Ruth Anne shook her head. "We'll be fine, Isabel."

"I'll go and get the midwife," Isabel said in a loud voice. "You need her now. That baby coming and coming soon."

Sophie burst into the cabin, "Ruth Anne honey, I's here."

Isabel smiled at her sister, then said, "Can

you please take Joshua to the chillun's house?"

While the slaves worked, the young ones were taken to the children's house to be under the care of elderly slave women who were of no more use in the house or fields.

Sophie nodded, then gave her a quick hug.

She gathered the children and led them out of the cabin.

Ruth Anne felt another contraction. Her baby was ready to leave her body and she was in an obliging mood, although she was weak.

Every time she tried to sit up, a wave of dizziness assailed her. Weary, Ruth Anne dropped back against the pillows of straw piled behind her. "Water…"

Sophie rushed to her side and gave her a few spoonfuls of cool water.

"George… where is he?"

"He outside looking powerful mad," Sophie stated. "He hate Mastah Joe something fierce, Ruth Anne."

"Could you go get him for me? I need to talk to George."

Sophie nodded. "I's be right back."

She walked over to the door and opened it, shouting for George to come inside.

He stormed into the house and over to where Ruth Anne lay. "You called for me?"

She nodded. "George, sit down here for a minute and let me talk to you."

She glanced over at her sister, who said, "I'll be right outside the door. Call me if you need me."

When they were alone, Isabel said, "I know you, George, and we don't need you stirring up a pot of trouble. We don't know if this baby is coming out light or dark skinned, but it's still my baby all the same."

George clenched his fists. "I hate that man," he uttered.

"I know that and I'm telling you to leave it be. Leave Mastah Joe to the Lawd. On Judgment day, he gonna have a lot to answer for. George honey, just hold onto that."

Pain ripped through Ruth Anne.

She reached for George's hand, gripping it tightly.

Ruth Anne struggled to catch her breath. "Lawd, please help me," she pleaded softly.

Chapter 10

Eleanor stirred.

"Mom look, she's moving," Julia stated, a look of complete surprise on her face. "Maybe we should we get the doctor."

Myra shook her head. "Ain't nothing they can do. She does that every now and then. Eleanor will move or get these strange expressions on her face as if she's going through something. After a while, she's quiets down again."

Julia reached over and touched Eleanor's hand. "Hey sweetie, I came by to tell you that we love you. Regardless of everything that's happened, we are family and we're going to be here for yo—"

Julia stopped short when Eleanor's body arched as if straining for some unknown reason, her face contorted in pain. She moaned softly.

Myra rushed to the door, flinging it open and called for a nurse.

"I think she's in pain," she told the woman when she arrived.

Myra gently wiped Eleanor's brow. "She's never made a sound like that before. I think she's fighting her way back to us."

The nurse checked her out and made notes to her chart. "She seems fine, Miss Myra. She might have been dreaming."

"Mom, what do you think Eleanor could be dreaming about?" Julia questioned. "I thought she looked like she was in agony. If she was dreaming, then it must have been a nightmare."

Myra nodded in agreement.

"Eleanor doesn't look as peaceful as she did before," Julia insisted as she continued to study her aunt's face.

Myra stared at Eleanor and said, "I just wish I knew where she was right now."

***

"Push!"

Ruth Anne opened her eyes to the midwife shouting for her to push. Assisted by two women, she leaned forward, disoriented with her environment and from the excruciating pain.

"C'mon, Ruth Anne. I see the head, but I need you to push if'n you gon' bring dis chile into the world."

Ruth Anne, in a weakened state, forced her body to work harder. She was more than ready to unleash this burden of giving life. She wanted to see her baby and hold it in her arms.

"Good girl."

She sighed in relief as the contraction ebbed away. Ruth Anne gloried briefly in the reprieve she had been given from the pain.

It didn't last long.

Another contraction hit, this one much harder than the last. Ruth Anne struggled to catch her breath and tried to take her mind off the pain. When she had Joshua, her labor had been nothing like this.

Ruth Anne could feel that the bed was soaked with her blood. She knew deep down that there was something wrong with her.

"G-George… where's George?"

"He's outside, chile. He's waitin' on you to push dis baby out your body."

Isabel entered the room, saying, "I'ma help you, Ruth Anne. We gon' get this bitty baby out."

Ruth Anne looked over at her sister. "It h-hurts so bad."

Isabel propped her up and said, "I's here now to help you. Let's get to doing…"

She braced herself behind Ruth Anne's head. "Push," Isabel shouted.

Her sister screamed and pushed with all her might. Ruth Anne glanced down in time to see a crying baby with ivory-colored skin emerge from her body.

The midwife handed the baby to Sophie for her first bath.

Ruth Anne's gaze traveled to where Isabel stood. "It's time," she mouthed.

Isabel pressed her cheek to Ruth Anne, before easing out of the room.

Sophie brought the baby to her.

She waited a long while before leaving for the big house to let the master know that a new slave had been brought into the world. They wanted to give Isabel a head start before anyone knew she was gone.

Ruth Anne's eyes traveled the room and locked eyes with George. It was obvious that he was struggling to fight back tears of rage at the sight of the baby—a baby that was much too light to be his child.

The room suddenly started spinning.

Ruth Anne tried to speak, but no words would come out. She stretched out her hand towards George before darkness overtook her.

Isabel set out with two women, a man and two brothers, using the stars in the sky as a guide to the north and their freedom.

The uncertainty of their fate and the dangers of their escape soon started to discourage the men. With blisters on their feet and a hungry stomach, they questioned their plan, then tried to convince her to turn around.

"If we turn 'round now, we can make it back before anyone know we gone."

"I can't turn around," she said. "They gonna sell me for sure. I will die right here tonight before I go back to that plantation."

The others in the group agreed.

After a few more miles, the young men became frightened and turned around, heading back to the plantation while she and the others kept running through the woods.

With the birth of Ruth Anne's daughter, they wouldn't be missed right away. If they were lucky, it would be early morning before anyone found out.

Filled with hope and a strong belief in God, Isabel looked up toward the sky, following the North Star.

"We gon' be free," she told the travelers. "We on the road to freedom."

While Isabel was running for her life, Ruth Anne lay in bed fighting for hers after giving birth to the child she conceived with Mastah Joe.

Sophie wiped her face with a wet cloth.

Ruth Anne opened her eyes. "George ..."

"He's outside," her sister told her. "You want me to get him?"

"The baby... where is the baby?" she managed.

"She's right here beside you." Sophie lowered her voice to a whisper. "Ruth Anne, she beautiful and... white. George, he ain't doing so well with the news. He powerful mad and talking crazy."

"Sophie, promise me... take care of the baby. Her name Gemma. Mastah Joe say if she a girl, then name her Gemma. George ain't gon' want nothing doing wit that chile 'cause she ain't his."

"Ruth Anne, don't you talk dis way. You gon' be fine. You jus weak, is all. Get some rest and you be jus fine."

"I'm bleeding, Sophie and it won't stop. They done tried everything. I can feel my life leaving my body with every ounce of my blood."

Tears filled Sophie's eyes. "You can't leave us, Ruth Anne. The children, they need you, especially little Gemma."

"Promise me."

Her sister nodded. "I promise to keep Gemma safe. Joshua too."

"George, he is angry with Mastah Joe. I fear for him—that he gon' try to kill Mastah. I need you to try to talk some sense into George."

"I don't know if George will hear me out. He powerful mad that Gemma not his. He say Mastah Joe gon' pay for what he done to you."

Ruth Anne was getting weaker by the moment. "Give me the baby," she whispered.

Sophie placed the infant in her arms.

"You still have milk?" Ruth Anne asked. Her sister had given birth a couple of weeks ago, but the baby was a stillborn.

Sophie nodded.

"You have to feed her." Ruth Anne eyed the sleeping infant in her arms. She was a gorgeous baby. It made her sad knowing that George would never accept her as his own child. He told her one time that his pappy had smothered the white child his mother delivered. George was twelve at the time. They all lied and said the baby had been born dead.

Ruth Anne feared that George would do the same to her daughter.

She grieved for her beautiful child. Mastah Joe Hicks would not count his daughter among his children either.

As far as the Hicks family was concerned, Gemma would just be one more mulatto slave on his plantation. Another piece of property that they owned.

Chapter 11

Isabel and her companions heard the dogs barking, and sped up their pace.

"We needs to get to the swamp," she told them.

Most times, slave owners didn't like to use dogs because it signaled to the runaways that they were on their trail. Mastah Joe only sent out the dogs when his slaves had been gone for hours.

Isabel and her companions had been gone for close to one night, which meant that the men had been looking for them all day long.

With horses and dogs, it would not take

them long to catch up to the group on foot.

They used snuff, sprinkling it on the ground to throw off their scent and confuse the dogs.

They quickened their pace and sprinted in a run, cutting through the heavy brush areas, heading towards the swamp areas.

The barking grew louder.

The dogs were getting closer, Belle thought silently.

Isabel and the others all jumped into a swamp.

They kept quiet and slowly waded over to a heavily wooded area. The slave catchers were so close to their hiding place that they could hear their conversation.

The riders were not really looking for them, Isabel considered. They were looking for slaves—any runaway slaves. Every day, slaves turned up missing, mostly heading north toward a life of freedom.

She had heard that slave catchers patrolled the forest and main roads, which is why they were traveling though wooded areas. It became treacherous when one of the dogs caught a whiff of their scent and strayed nearby.

Isabel closed her eyes and prayed.

The dog inched closer and closer.

She watched as the fog seemed to take shape—the form of a woman.

Ziraili.

The dog suddenly started to howl as if scared and ran away.

"He must have found something," she heard one of the slave catchers holler. "Let's go."

Back in the slave quarters, Ruth Anne smiled at Ziraili before she passed peacefully into eternity.

Belva stopped by Eleanor's hospital room. She walked in with a beautiful bouquet of flowers. "I thought this would brighten up the room some."

Myra agreed.

"Eleanor must be feeling better today," Belva said. "She's smiling."

Myra turned away from the window in the hospital room. "Oh Lordy… she sure is—She's got a smile on her face."

"You look exhausted, Nana. Why don't you go home and get some rest?" she suggested. "I'll sit with her a while."

Before she could protest, Belva added, "Nana, it won't do you any good to get sick."

"How are you feeling?"

Smiling, Belva responded, "This is a good day."

A lone tear rolls down Myra's face. "I'm afraid to leave her," she confessed. "Winston's abandoned her. I'd never forgive myself if something happened and she …"

Belva embraced her grandmother. "Nothing is going to happen to Eleanor. We have to stand on God's word. That's what you've always told me, Nana. Well, now is the time to stand. I know that God is going to heal me of cancer. He's going to heal Eleanor, too. I have faith and I'm standing on His word."

"You're right, sugar. You sho' telling the truth."

"Just go home and get a good night's sleep. Vincent will bring you back in the morning. Nana, I know what you're trying to do. You'll get your chance with Eleanor. I really believe that, but you have to take care of yourself."

Myra shook her head no. "Belva, I'ma go home for a couple of hours, but I'm coming back," she stated in a tone that brooked no argument. "Every night that my sister is here in this hospital, I'm gonna be here, too."

Belva broke into a grin. "Yes ma'am. I hear you."

Myra planted a kiss on Eleanor's forehead before grabbing her purse. "Honey, I'll be right back. I'm just going home for a little while. I promise you I'll be back here before you know that I'm gone."

"Don't forget your Bible," Belva said.

"Put it in bed with Eleanor. I want her to feel its power." She stifled a yawn. "Belva honey, I'll be back in a little while."

"Vincent's outside. He'll take you home."

Myra nodded. "If you need to call me—don't wait. Call me, Belva."

"I will, Nana."

Myra hummed a hymn softly as she slowly made her way down the hospital corridor.

The slave hunters eventually gave up and decided to turn around, heading back to the main paths. If there were anything to be found, the dogs would have sniffed it out already.

Isabel and her companions breathed a sigh of relief. They remained in the swamp for a few more hours, fearful that the white riders would come back.

When Isabel felt that it was safe to continue their journey, they sought shelter in the thick brush areas.

Days turned into a week and the companions found the journey long and strenuous, but they were determined to make it to freedom. Malnourishment and exhaustion took a heavy toll on their bodies, but still they forged ahead.

They traveled by night and during the day; hid in the forests and swamps.

Isabel had a deep down feeling that Ruth Anne was gone, and grieved the loss of her dear sister.

Ruth Anne had been dead a couple of weeks.

Sophie visited the grave whenever she could sneak away from the big house. She sat down on the ground, her eyes wet with tears.

"Ruth Anne, I miss you so much. I wish you was here to see your little girl. She gettin' bigger and bigger every day."

Sophie wiped at her eyes. "That George… he a handful. He been talking crazy talk." She stole a quick peek over her shoulder before whispering, "He say he gon' kill Mastah Joe." She nodded. "He sho' did…"

George was a deeply Christian man fired by religious indignation against slavery and the Old Testament with emphasis on the delivery of the children of Israel freed from bondage in Egypt.

From the moment, Joe Hicks had forced himself on Ruth Anne, George began to make plans to attack his owner. He had other slaves enlisted to join him in his revolt. They had planned to gather late at night, start a major fire and when the white men came out their doors, he and his men would kill them with axes, picks, or guns—whatever they could get their hands on. They would then enter the houses and kill all the occupants.

All his followers, ten of them, were filled with anger just like George. Their master had allowed his overseer to abuse one of the men so much that his body was covered with scars and his hunger for revenge unquenched. They planned to execute the master and all his family members. Then, they planned to move from house-to-house throughout the night executing every white person they could find.

She sighed, then said, "That man gon' git hisself killed—that's what gon' happen."

Sophie rose to her feet, slapping the dirt off her dress. "Missus probably throwing a hissy fit right about now if'n she can't find me. I best be on my way back to the big house."

She was halfway down the road, when a strange sensation stopped her in her tracks. Sophie could not explain the feeling. She glanced over her shoulder, her eyes searching.

In the early morning mist, it looked like someone was standing over the mound of dirt where Ruth Ann was buried. She heard all the stories growing up and knew that the woman fit the description of her great-great-grandmother Ziraili.

Sophie felt a chill snake down her spine. When she looked a second time, there was no one there. She broke into a run.

Chapter 12

It was pouring down heavy rain. Isabel and her companions found a large tree and sought its protection after a long night of walking. They were all tired and wanted to get some sleep for a few hours before moving on.

Raymond, one of the men pretended to be asleep. Hs eyes traveled, searching out their surroundings.

When he figured they were all sleeping, he got up to leave. He thought it best to travel alone. Raymond was deathly afraid of getting caught.

In his haste, he stepped on a piece of wood,

snapping it.

"Wha—"Jeff got up and rushed off after his brother with Isabel in pursuit.

"You gon' mess 'round and get us all kilt," she grumbled.

Isabel tripped and fell to the ground, cutting her knee. She quickly covered up the blood with dirt and rocks, then tore off a piece of her dress and made a bandage.

Isabel walked, following the path that Raymond and his brother took, but then she heard voices—voices she didn't recognize.

She hid behind a fallen tree.

A group of slave catchers surrounded Jeff and Raymond. The overseer from the Gerard plantation was with them.

"Where's the witch?" the Overseer questioned. "Isabel. Where is she? Where are the others?"

"Suh, ain't nobody out here but me and Raymond," Jeff responded. "Only us."

"Boy, you telling me that it's just the two of you that left the plantation?"

"Yessum. That's what I telling you. We ain't seen no other folks."

Isabel chewed on her bottom lip as she tried

to think of a way to save them, but the dire truth was that there wasn't anything that Isabel could do to save her companions.

The men's fate was in the hands of God.

She'd gestured for the others to make their way to the river.

Isabel moved quietly, careful not to step on anything that would draw attention to her. She heard what sounded like a bird squawking.

It was a signal from the others that they'd made it across the river. She hastened to join them.

Jeff carried his brother along the long dusty road leading back to the Hicks plantation. His body was weak and famished; his neck burning from being pulled by the noose around his neck.

They had been traveling for days, suffering cruel treatments at the hand of the overseer and slave catchers.

Two other runaway slaves had been discovered, although they didn't belong to Hicks. Jeff was glad that Isabel and the others had escaped.

He prayed for their safety. He and Raymond had lied about not knowing where the others went. They would never betray Isabel, so they both swore it had been just the two of them running away.

Jeff was relieved by the time they reached the slave quarters.

He dropped to his knees in sheer exhaustion. Several slaves including George rushed over to hem. Their mother burst into loud sobs when she saw Raymond's condition.

George and Jeff's gazes met and held.

The overseer grabbed Jeff and shoved him towards a nearby tree while George and a couple of the men picked up the severely wounded Raymond and carried him into the cabin.

Unaware of what his fate will be, Jeff found himself yanked to his feet and cuffed.

He took no thought of himself, but of Raymond and his injuries. His brother had always been hot-headed, and refused to go down without a fight, which resulted in one of the buckra slave catchers shooting him in the gut.

Jeff knew his brother would not live much longer. The only comfort he found in the loss of a life was that his brother would finally be free.

His thoughts scattered as he felt the cutting sting of the whip. The overseer wanted to make an example of Jeff and Raymond, so that the other slaves would be too afraid to run.

Jeff bite his bottom lip until blood ran down his chin. He was in excruciating pain but refused to cry out. He would not let the buckra win.

Tonight, they would die by the hands of slaves. George and some of the other slaves had conspired to take over the plantation.

He would've preferred to have been miles away as the massacre unfolded. He'd heard of other attempts such as these and believed that nothing good could come out of it. Any slaves caught would be hung. There would be no winners.

Sophie rinsed out the blood in a bucket of water, turning it bright red. Ma Sue packed the wound with cobwebs and other remedies to try to stop the bleeding, but nothing she tried worked.

She removed his trousers and gasped in surprise.

"Raymond," Sophie whispered an hour later when she returned to check his wound. "Can you hear me?"

He moaned and muttered something she did not understand.

"What happened to Isabel?"

Raymond shook his head from side to side. He moaned a second time.

Sophie sent up a quick prayer for her sister's safety.

"F-Free..." Raymond grunted. His voice was barely above a whisper.

"Huh?" she responded.

Sophie bent down low over Raymond. "Are you saying that Isabel is free? She and the others was able to get away from the slave catchers?"

He tried to nod, but even the slightest movement caused him pain.

Raymond convulsed and then suddenly, his body went still.

Sophie ran to the door and called for Ma Sue to come check on the dying man.

"Is he..." Sophie couldn't finish her sentence.

Raymond's mother began to cry, ripping at her dress.

"He's not dead," Ma Sue announced. "But it won't be long now. He's lost too much blood."

"Why'd they haft to kill my boy?" his mother questioned. "Lawd, when you gon' come save us?"

Ma Sue rushed over to Raymond's mother who was becoming more and more hysterical by the minute, and screaming out curses against the buckra.

They tried to quiet her. She could get them all whipped with the things she was saying in her grief.

Raymond died later that day and was quickly buried by some of the other slaves.

Sophie eased over to where Jeff was cuffed to give him the news. "I'm sorry."

Jeff's eyes filled with unshed tears. "He free now."

Amid the confusion of Raymond's death and Jeff's whipping, George and his co-conspirators saw this as an opportunity to slay Hicks.

They waited patiently for it to get dark, then covered themselves in mud.

The first mission was to burn down the house.

Soon smoke filled the sky, feeding on the wind as fiery tendrils spread angrily, scorching and burning everything in its path, including some of the slave cabins.

When the mistress and master of the plantation came running out, George planted his axe in the man's head while one of the other men stabbed his wife to death.

A couple of slaves tied the overseer to a tree and whipped him until he begged for the one thing he would never give them—mercy.

Other slaves began burning down the cabins in the slave quarters.

Sophie grabbed Joshua and just as she was about to walk over to where Gemma lay sleeping, the roof fell, blocking her path.

She frantically tried to get to Gemma, but the burning debris prevented her from doing so. Joshua's fearful cries caught her attention and reminded her that they were in danger.

Sophie picked up Joshua and left the house. She spotted Ma Sue outside and handed the boy to her.

"I needs to go back in that cabin," Sophie said, growing hysterical with each passing moment. "I gotta get the baby. I promised my sister that I wouldn't let no harm come to that chile. I needs to get Gemma."

"It's too late, chile," one of the other women told her. "That place done burned down to the ground."

Sophie screamed at the top of her lungs and had to be restrained as she tried to run back into that burning house. She took little comfort in the fact that Gemma was with her mother now.

Chapter 13

Jeff had worked one hand out of the cuff, but could not free the other one. He glanced around until he spotted an ax laying a few feet away.

Ignoring the pain, Jeff manipulated his body enough until he was able to grab it with his free hand.

He stared at his hand in the cuff, lifted the ax over his head and closed his eyes. He blocked out what he was about to do in his mind.

His scream of agony ripped through the night, sending chills into all who heard it.

George and his renegade slaves ran toward the woods while the others who were too afraid to leave, went off in the other direction, heading for a neighboring plantation. They did not dare stay around for fear that they would be blamed for what happened.

When the owners at the next plantation discovered what had happened, they were frightened, but allowed Sophie along with Ma Sue, a few of the other women and children inside a locked barn.

Sophie had a bad feeling when a group of men took the male slaves off somewhere.

Ma Sue swore she heard gunshots and burst into tears.

Sophie held Joshua close to her chest. "Lawd, please send your guardian angels to watch over us," she prayed.

"Us need you real bad, Lawd," another woman added. "Please doan let them white folk come back heh to kill us. Us ain't done nothing."

"They got us locked up in here like animals," Ma Sue whispered.

"They gon' burn us alive," another slave said before bursting into tears.

Fighting back her own grief, Sophie tried to keep everybody calm. She wanted to cry, but no tears would come because she was too consumed with fear.

"They wouldn't have taken the men away if they was gonna kill us," she said after a moment. "They scared like us. You know there's slaves out there killing the white folk. They don't wanna be murdered in they sleep, and if locking the barn door help them to feel safe— it don't bother me."

"What us gon' do?" someone asked. "We can't go back to the plantation, can we?"

"I don't know," Sophie stated. "Just lie down and try to get some sleep. We'll see what comes with morning."

She found a corner and sat down with her arms wrapped around her knees. Sophie could not contain her tears any longer.

Gemma was like a daughter to her and Sophie felt like she had lost another child. Sophie held the Bible to her chest and closed her eyes.

She woke up at the slightest sound. Sophie reached over to make sure Joshua was still beside her. She could not bear to lose him, too.

When morning came, the owners of the

plantation told them that they could stay there until relatives of the Hicks family could be contacted. If none were found, an auction would be held and they would be sold.

While picking cotton, Sophie sensed that someone was nearby, watching her.

Fear snaked down her spine as her eyes quickly surveyed her surroundings. "I know you're here," she said as calmly as she could manage. Sophie found a huge stick nearby and picked it up.

She would not go down without a fight.

"Sophie…"

She was too afraid to respond and she did not recognize the voice.

A woman materialized from behind a tree. "I have Gemma and she needs you, Sophie. Her mother is gone and you are all she has."

After a moment, Sophie emerged from a thicket of bushes. "Who are you?" she asked her. "And how do you know my name?"

Instead of answering her questions, the woman held out the baby to Sophie as she walked up to her. "You have to go," she urged. "The others are near the water. They're waiting for you. *Go now.*"

"I feels like I know you," she murmured, searching her memory.

"You must go," the woman insisted. "Take the baby."

Sophie relieved the woman of the sleeping child and turned to leave. She stopped a few yards later and looked over her shoulder.

The woman was gone. Then the realization dawned on her. She was the same woman she'd seen at her sister's grave.

Ziraili.

Had she been talking to a ghost?

Unnerved, Sophie ran quickly through the forest, holding the baby close to her heart.

Weary, Isabel and her companions made it to the first house on their path to freedom. There, they were placed into a wagon, covered with a sack and driven to the next destination.

When they arrived at the second stop, one of the women with her fell ill and was unable to travel with them to the next destination.

She released a long sigh of relief when they successfully made it to Philadelphia where she met William Still, a stationmaster on the Underground Railroad.

During her journey, Isabel realized the call placed on her heart and decided that she would not only go back to get her sister and the babies, but that she would join the Underground Railroad to help others. The seed was planted the moment she first listened to her sister read from the Old Testament.

After sharing this with Still, he invited her to work with members of the Philadelphia Anti-Slavery Society to learn about the workings of the Underground Railroad.

Isabel soon joined the already, functioning Underground Railroad on the Eastern Shore, traveling by night. With instructions from white and black stationmasters, she began helping other slaves escape to freedom.

Time and time again, she made successful visits to Maryland on the Underground Railroad. In December 1857, Isabel made her final trip to Maryland. This time, she planned on bringing Sophie and the children back to Philadelphia with her. From there, they would travel to Canada.

***

Mastah Hicks' brother came up from Virginia and settled into the big house. The slaves returned, and soon found he was intent on avenging the deaths of his brother and sister-in-law.

He was a cruel master and none of his newly acquired slaves liked him. Plans to run away were rampant along the slave grapevine. Sophie heard word that Isabel would be coming to escort them up north and stealthily began making preparations.

Runaway slaves that had been captured and returned to the plantation were brutally punished by her master. Their feet were chopped off to prevent future escapes and they were branded on the face or hand with the letter "R" for runaway.

The new master had come to Sophie's cabin for the last two nights, abusing her violently. He beat her the first night when she tried to refuse him. Sophie feared he would kill her if she didn't run away.

The night finally arrived for them to leave. Sophie was afraid that the owner would come to her cabin and find her gone, but earlier in the day, he had fallen off his horse and suffered a broken leg.

They left when night was at its darkest, remaining careful to stay in the shadows. Sophie gave Gemma and Joshua an herbal potion to keep them quiet.

They quietly made their way to a house where they would be hiding in an attic over the barn for the next two weeks. It had been predetermined that they would stay here until they were supposed to meet up with Isabel on Christmas night.

The slave grapevine had been ripe with tales of how dear sweet Isabel had come to Maryland and escorted scores of slaves to freedom.

Sophie felt a sense of pride when she thought of Isabel and her bravery. One day, she would tell Joshua and Gemma of their mother's sacrifice and the courage of their aunt Isabel.

Myra rose to her feet and began to pace as she continued her story.

"Early February, Isabel arrived safely in

Philadelphia with six passengers, three of whom were Sophie, Joshua, and Gemma. Now don't nobody know what happened to George and those other men that night. What we do know is that a Quaker family and members of the Underground Railroad helped Sophie and the children settle down in Canada."

Myra heard footsteps and turned around to find Winston standing in the doorway. "What you want?" she asked. "You here to see if she dead?"

"She's my wife."

"She's been your wife the whole time she's been in this hospital," Myra stated. "She was your wife when you were out in the streets running 'round on her."

Winston opened his mouth to speak, but she cut him off. "Don't bother denying it. You'll only make yourself look like a fool. I'm not talking 'bout what I heard... I know you've cheated on Eleanor. More than once."

"And she's been so upstanding? I may have been unfaithful, but I was the one deceived in this marriage."

Myra shook her head. "If you're here to play the victim, then you might as well leave.

Eleanor doesn't need to hear this mess."

"I'm here because I am concerned about her."

She didn't respond.

"Eleanor and I have been married for over 40 years. We had a lot of good times together."

"No need to tell me," Myra uttered. "Your words don't mean nothing to me. Save them for Eleanor."

Chapter 14

Sophie was filled with joy when she discovered that Jeff was among the next group of slaves that had made it to Canada. She happily welcomed him into her home, then asked about his hand.

"I cut it off that night. I didn't wanna burn in that fire. It was spreading quick. I ain't have no other choice."

"Do you know what happened to George?"

Jeff nodded. "He was shot by the overseer from one of the other plantations. I heard that it was ol' evil Snipes from Lafayette Plantation, but I's not real sure on that account."

"Well, I'm so glad that you made it here." Sophie smiled. She had always liked Jeff, but worried that he'd gotten himself killed. He had been long gone when the new master took over the plantation.

Grinning, he said, "We's free now."

"Yes, we are," she responded.

She landed a job as a domestic while the old woman next door watched the children for her. Jeff did whatever odd jobs he could find, pushing past his handicap.

Sophie and Jeff's friendship turned to love.

They married a short time later and added two more children to their family.

Gemma met Henri Toussaint in 1874.

It didn't take much persuasion on his part to get her to come to New Orleans. She was completely in love with him. She thought he was extremely handsome and exciting. More than anything, he made her feel like a queen.

Henri came from a very wealthy family with ties to French royalty.

"Any children we have will be educated in

France," he promised her. "They will be given my name."

He even purchased a house for her on Rue de Rampart.

Gemma thought it perfect. *I'm going to have a cook, maids and boys to make messages.* Her friend, Marie used a couple of boys to run errands, fetch fruits and wines from the French Market. Sometimes she sent them for silks and threads on Royal Street.

Gemma thought about all of the beautiful silk dresses she would own, although during the day she could only wear simple cotton gowns, but in the evenings, she was free to wear her silks and satins.

She was excited about starting her new life with Henri.

Six months later, Henri was dead.

Gemma was distraught when Francis sent her away. She walked into the house, removing the tignon that was twisted about her head and knotted. An ordinance made it an offense for *femmes de couleur* to walk around in silk, jewels, or plumes. To do so, would put her at risk for being whipped like a slave, so she kept her head covered whenever she was out in public.

Her long, curly hair fell loosely around her heart-shaped face.

She remembered all the fun they had attending concerts and plays. Gemma dabbed at her wet cheeks with her sleeves.

She heard footsteps and turned around. "Marie... Henri's dead! He's gone. My Henri's gone! What am I going to do? What can I do?"

Her friend rushed to her side, hugging her. "Honey, I'm so sorry."

"Someone killed him. They shot him straight in the heart."

She rocked Gemma gently from side to side. "I'm so very sorry."

Her teeth clattered.

Marie walked her upstairs to the bedroom.

Once she had Gemma settled in bed, she said, "I think you should come stay with me."

Gemma shook her head. "I want to be home. I need to feel close to Henri."

"I'm going to have Big John come stay with you. I want to make sure you're safe."

Her eyes grew wide with fright. "Do you

think they were trying kill me?"

"*Non*," Marie quickly responded. "But I don't want to take any chances. Now, try to sleep. You've had a trying day."

Gemma closed her eyes but sleep evaded her.

She laid there for a couple of hours, then got up. She guessed that Henri was probably in a coffin by now.

Marie burst through the door. "I thought I heard you stirring." She stepped into the hallway and called out, "Mary, come to the bedroom."

When the young woman arrived, Gemma said, "Prepare a bath for me."

She noticed that Marie had covered the mirror as was their custom when mourning. She knew the front door would be draped with a dark cloth as well.

Gemma stepped into the tub of bathwater that her maid prepared and bathed.

Afterward, she dressed in black, then braided her hair, wrapping it into a bun at her nape.

She joined Marie downstairs.

"I had Mary make you some sassafras tea."

At the mention of her name, the maid entered the parlor carrying a fine tea service.

Gemma sank down on the sofa and accepted the cup from Mary.

Marie joined her. She sipped from her teacup. "Mary, this is delicious. You need to teach my Sally how to make a proper cup of tea."

"Why, thank you, "Miss Marie."

She could hear someone knocking on the door.

Mary rushed to see to her unexpected guest.

Henri's brother strode into the room. He gave a polite nod in Marie's direction.

"Hello Francis."

"I just left my parents. Mother took to her bed and my father… he didn't take it well either."

Gemma nodded in understanding.

"A drunk shot into the crowd," Francis said. "My brother's death is a tragic accident."

"Are you sure?"

"There were witnesses. The man is in jail." He paused a moment, then said, "My parents are returning to Paris after Henri's funeral. Mother longs to be near her family. Henri's wife has a decided to remain here in New Orleans."

"Is there something more," Gemma asked,

noting the hesitancy in his voice.

"Father requests that you not attend the funeral."

His request did not come as a surprise to Gemma. She knew that Henri's wife would never allow her presence at the service for fear of being humiliated in front of family and friends.

"I wonder if he ever really loved me," she whispered. "Was I just someone he used to satisfy his lust?"

"Where is this coming from?" Francis asked. "You know Henri loved you."

"I know that's what he said."

"The pearls that my brother gave you," Francis said, "they have been in our family since the 1700's. The French King Renaud II gave them to my four times great-grandmother Princess Elyse. Henri gave them to you and not his *wife*."

"I'm pregnant," she announced. "I never got the chance to tell Henri." Tears rolled down her cheeks. "I don't know what to do."

He embraced her. "You don't have to worry about anything, dear sweet Gemma. I promise."

She wasn't sure what Francis could do, but

she was grateful for any help he could give her.

Chapter 15

The day after Henri Toussaint was laid to rest in Lafayette Cemetery, Gemma visited his grave.

"My love," she said. "They wouldn't let me attend your funeral, but I'm here now. I miss you so much." Gemma paused a moment before saying, "I'm pregnant. There will always be a part of you with me."

She laid her hand on the mound of dirt. "I still can't believe that you're gone. I miss you so much. I heard that you were killed by some drunk who decided to shoot into a crowd of people… they found the man and he's in jail."

Gemma sighed. "I take no comfort in that because it doesn't bring you back to me."

She left the cemetery and went to her friend's house.

Marie fed her red beans and rice while they talked about Gemma's plans for the future.

"I will be fine," she said. "Henri left me quite a bit of money. His brother said he would be here to help me as well."

Marie met her gaze. "In what way?"

"I don't know, but I appreciate the offer."

"I've always believed that boy was in love with you, Gemma. I've seen the way he watches you."

"He's been a good friend to me, Marie."

"I tell you true. That boy loves you. It's not a bad thing, Gemma. You're having a baby and you need a man. With his help, you might be able to keep your house. I'm sure Henri's widow will try to take it from you."

She considered Marie's words. "I hadn't thought about losing my home."

"When Edward died, his widow came and told Anna that she had an hour to get out and to only take her personal belongings. She wasn't allowed to take any of the gifts he had given her."

"If only they had been allowed to marry."

"Paul lied and said that he had black blood," Marie said in a low whisper. "It's the only reason we were able to get married."

"It's not true?"

Marie shook her head. "We were determined to be together."

Gemma sighed. "Even if the laws were different, Henri and I still couldn't marry. He already has a wife."

"Francis does not," Marie reminded her.

Gemma smiled. "No, he does not, but he comes from a very important family. We could never say he is of mixed race."

"No, but he can be a very powerful protector. He has influence, Gemma. Francis is everything you need."

Gil Henri Toussaint entered the world red-faced and screaming.

Mary bathed the baby before handing him to Gemma. "He's beautiful, Missus."

Gemma smiled. "Yes, he is…"

Francis peeked into the room. "Can I come in?"

"Of course."

"It's a boy," Mary said.

He walked over to the bed and planted a kiss on Gemma's forehead. "He looks like Henri."

She nodded. "I think so, too."

When Henri died, Gemma wasn't sure she would ever recover, and while she missed him—she had found a way to survive.

Marie had been right about Francis. He declared his feelings shortly after Henri's death. Although she felt some affection toward him, Gemma wasn't in love with Francis.

The more time they spent together, her feelings evolved into love.

He was a good man and like his brother, Francis treated Gemma like a queen.

Two years later, she gave birth to a daughter. She and Francis also had three sons, all of whom where educated abroad. Their marriage lasted until her death at the age of 96. Francis died at the old age of 101.

***

A wave of dizziness washed over Myra, forcing her to sit down in the chair beside Eleanor's bed.

An orderly brought her some food, but she wasn't hungry.

She settled back in the chair and closed her eyes, attempting to get some sleep after a restless night.

Belva came out to the hospital to stay with Eleanor while Myra went home to shower and change clothes.

"Mom, I'm worried about you," Theresa said when she picked her up. "You don't look well."

She dismissed her concern with a wave of her hand. "You don't have to worry about me. I'm fine."

"Mom, are you taking your meds?"

Myra nodded. "Theresa, I'm okay." She was tired of everyone fussing over her.

"Did you eat something?"

"They brought a tray in for me this morning." She didn't both mentioning that she hadn't touched it.

"I'm going to stop over here and get you

something."

"Theresa…"

"Mama, you hate hospital food," she stated as she pulled into the parking lot of a fast food restaurant.

Myra had no concern for her own life. She couldn't exactly explain how she knew, but that she would be just fine. She had to be there for Eleanor.

Chapter 16

M yra stretched and yawned.

"This chair isn't really all that comfortable," she told Eleanor in a loud whisper. "But I appreciate having a chair to sit in at all."

She heard footsteps and glanced over her shoulder to see if anyone were coming into the room.

No one did.

Myra returned her attention back to Eleanor. "I guess I'll get back to telling you our history. "After Gemma was born, Francis and Gemma added a girl and three boys to their family. All of them were educated abroad. They were married a long time. Gil grew up to be a fine man. He went to Scotland for his degree and became a doctor. When he returned to America, Gil set up a medical practice in New York. Francis Jr. studied law. He died of pneumonia before he could graduate though."

Myra rose to her feet. She needed to stand for a while to keep her circulation moving. She continued her story when she sat down minutes later. "Gemma's daughter, Leona married a Native American and moved out west somewhere. Her youngest son, Piers followed in his brother's footsteps and became a doctor as well. He returned to New Orleans and was a staff doctor at an orphanage."

Myra continued to recount the family history to an unconscious Eleanor, because it keep her from worrying. "In the fall of 1920, Piers became a grandfather for the first time. His grandson was named Bernard Gaston Toussaint."

"Bernard is our great-grandfather. You won't remember him because he left Granny before we were born. You see Granny devoted most of her energy to serving the Lord. She didn't have any time for family."

Myra reached over and took Eleanor's hand. "You look a lot like Granny. She was a beautiful woman and she had pretty hands just like yours."

A nurse walked into the room to check Eleanor's vitals.

Myra used this time to go to the bathroom to relieve her bladder.

She winced in pain. Her back hurt something fierce from spending all that time in that chair.

When she came out of the bathroom, Myra sat down and began again. "Now, where did I leave off…"

The edges of darkness disappeared and Eleanor found herself standing in front of a dark wooden casket. The man in the death sleep looked familiar although Eleanor had never met him.

It did not take her long to realize that he was her great-grandfather, Bernard. She had seen a picture of him in one of the family photo albums.

"Remy," she heard someone say. They were speaking to her, Eleanor realized. She turned, catching a fleeting glimpse of Ziraili before she vanished into nothingness.

Eleanor now understood whenever she caught sight of Ziraili, she was about to experience the life of yet another ancestor. This time it was her grandfather. This was the first time she'd inhabited the body of a man.

"I'm so sorry for your loss," one of the visitors whispered in his ear. "Your daddy was a real nice man."

"That's what I hear," Remy responded. He hadn't seen the man in years.

His father was hit by a car driven by a white man. Bernard was walking across the street to go to the store when the driver refused to stop and just ran him down. His death was labeled an accident, but it was murder as far as the black folk were concerned.

Remy glanced over his shoulder to where his mother was seated. Friends and family gathered around her, offering food, tissues and other comforts for the grieving widow. He shook his head when he heard his mother say, "I'm fine. Rest won't change a thing," she responded. "Bernard's gone."

"He's been gone a long time," Remy uttered under his breath. "He left you years ago and you acting like it was a few days ago." He was looking forward to leaving in a couple of days to attend college in California. He wanted to get as far away from her mother as possible. All she cared about was trying to save his soul.

All Remy cared about was music. He had been playing the saxophone since he was six years old.

His mother walked up to the casket. "You never respected him," she stated, her tone accusing. "He was a wonderful doctor. He followed the same path as your grandfather—his father."

Rebecca Toussaint was a tall, full-figured woman with warm brown eyes and a pretty smile. She wasn't a bad person—just had her priorities mixed up. Remy loved his mother, but he resented that she had not been very supportive of his dreams and aspirations.

"And look where it got him."

Rebecca turned toward him, her arms folded across her chest. "You are going to have to forgive him, Remy. If you expect God to forg—"

"Mom," he said, cutting her off. "I don't need you preaching to me right now."

Rebecca sighed and nodded. "Fine. It's your salvation."

Remy walked out of the room, leaving his mother alone with his father's casket.

He went upstairs to his room.

"I can't wait to get out of here." Remy pulled open a drawer and began putting clothes into a suitcase. In just a few days, he would be thousands of miles away from his mother and her preaching.

He was looking forward to the freedom to do whatever he wanted—sleep in later, drink alcohol, smoke... whatever he wanted.

Later that evening, Rebecca peeked into his room. "I have something for you."

Remy shifted into a sitting position on the bed.

She handed him a Bible. "Keep this with you always."

He covered his disappointment with a pasted on smile. "Thank you, Mama."

"Are you sure about this decision to go all the way to California for school. Your dad made sure that you would be able to attend any college you want."

"I *want* to go to Berkeley."

"I see," she responded, although Remy could tell that she really didn't understand his decision.

"I never stopped loving your father," Rebecca blurted. "Even though we weren't living in the same house—I always knew that he would be here if I needed him. Now that he's gone, I don't know how I can make it without him," she murmured.

Remy took her hand in his. "If you believe what you're always telling me, then you and Dad will see each other again in Heaven. Dad wouldn't want you walking around feeling this way. He'd want you to go on with your life."

Rebecca nodded. "You're right. I always thought I'd be the one to go first. It's just like your daddy to run off and meet Jesus first."

One month later, Remy strolled around the college campus, humming softly. He hadn't seen much, but enough to fall in love with California.

A young woman with sun-kissed blond hair and clear blue eyes approached him.

"Hey Baby," she said.

"Megan, I'm glad you're here. I need some help with this history assignment. You think you can meet me after your last class?"

"Of course."

He kissed her. "That's my girl."

Remy met Megan on the first day of class. They hit it off immediately. He'd initially debated on whether to tell her about his African American blood for fear she'd drop him on the spot.

After deciding that honesty was the best approach—he told her the truth. Megan didn't flinch and confessed that she'd suspected as much.

"I don't care about skin color," she'd said, "but since we're discussing this… I need to tell you that my parents would have a fit if they knew I was dating a colored man."

"I can believe that with you being from Mississippi and all."

She gave him a playful punch in the arm. "Not all of us are prejudiced, cause if we were, then people like you wouldn't exist."

Remy chuckled. "I guess you're right about that."

He walked Megan to class, then sprinted to his own. He didn't dare be late.

Myra left Eleanor alone at the hospital when she heard that Belva wasn't feeling well. She walked into her house, heading straight to Belva's room.

"Those treatments make her sick," Julia said.

"But they're killing the cancer."

"I've been reading about the benefits of natural alternatives. I'm going to talk to her doctor. I read that they could lessen some of the side effects of the chemo therapy."

"Julia, I think that's a good idea."

"How's Eleanor doing?"

"The same."

"Have you heard any more from Winston?" Julia inquired.

Myra shook her head.

"It's a shame... the way he's treating her."

She agreed. "Julia, I've been thinking about this for a while… we need to make sure that Belva has the wedding of her dreams. Where's that book of hers? We need to get busy."

"Here it is," her said, picking it up off a nearby shelf.

"She picked out what she wanted her wedding cake to look like—we need to get it ordered," Myra said. "I have one more fitting for my dress. I still need to find the perfect pair of shoes."

"What about the pearls?"

"I'll get them from Winston if I have to," Myra responded. "Belva's wearing the Toussaint pearls."

Julia typed notes into her cell phone. "I'll check with Vincent to make sure the groomsmen all have their tuxedos ordered."

Belva stirred in bed. She opened her eyes. "Nana… what are y'all doing?"

"We're making sure everything is on track for the wedding."

She smiled, then sat up in bed. "I need to reschedule my fitting from tomorrow to next week. Mama, can you call the boutique?"

"Sure, sweetie."

Belva eyed her engagement ring. "I can't wait to marry Vincent. Oh, I didn't tell y'all. He got accepted into law school."

Myra throw up her hands and did a little dance. "Praise the Lord. I knew he would get in. Hallelujah."

"That's wonderful news," Julia said. "We going to have a lawyer in the family. We got doctors, a pharmacist and a dentist."

Myra returned to the hospital a short time after six o' clock.

She stood beside Eleanor's bed and said, "You're gonna be just fine." Myra knew there was power in the tongue and as long as she had breathe in her body, she was going to speak life and healing over both Belva and Eleanor.

Chapter 17

Six months after he left for college, Rebecca was surprised to find her son standing on the porch with luggage when she opened her front door. She had been expecting her next-door neighbor to come over to indulge in a slice of freshly baked lemon pound cake.

"Remy, oh my goodness! What in the world …"

"I realized that I really missed you and I wanted to come home. I hope it's okay with you."

Rebecca embraced her son. "Of course it's okay. I'm so glad to have you home. To tell the truth, I've been plumb worried since you left New Orleans. Did you transfer to a college down here?"

Remy walked into the house carrying two suitcases. "I knew you were worried. You always tried to hide it, but I knew. I could tell from the way you talked." He glanced around the room. "I'm so glad to be home."

His words pleased Rebecca greatly.

"The first thing I intend to do is get a job," he announced. "I'm gonna go looking tomorrow."

Rebecca gave a short laugh. "You don't have to hit the ground running, Remy. You just got here, but what about school?"

"I wanna work, Mama. I don't think school's for me. Not right now anyway." He paced across the living room floor. "I want to work for a while, then figure out the rest."

Rebecca eyed her son. "Is everything okay, Remy? You seem nervous."

He sat down. "Mama, I need to tell you something."

"What is it, baby?"

"I'm going to be a daddy," he announced.
She gasped. "Say what?"

"I want to get married, Mama. That's why I need to find a job, so Megan and I can get married and prepare for the baby."

"I suppose it's the right thing to do, but I sent you to California to get an education—not a baby."

"Mama, I know that. It's not like I planned on this happening. It did and I'm not gonna run from my responsibility."

"So where is this girl?"

"She still in California. She'll come here as soon as I get a job and find a place for us to live."

"Son, you and Megan can live here."

Remy stood up and gave his mother another hug. "Thank you."

"I'm so glad you're home," Rebecca said. Deep down, she was disappointed that he'd allowed himself to get mixed up with some girl, taking his focus off school. She wanted so much more for her son.

Megan arrived three weeks later.

Rebecca had hoped that Remy would find

a nice girl within his own race to marry, but no—he had to find a white girl with parents who hated blacks. The poor girl had been disowned and forbidden to contact her family unless she placed the baby for adoption or left it with Rebecca and Remy.

Megan refused.

The day of their wedding, Rebecca was up early and dressed when Megan ventured downstairs.

"You look beautiful," she told Megan when she walked into the kitchen. "Would you like something to eat?"

"No thank you, Mrs. Toussaint. I'm too nervous to eat right now."

The simple white dress Megan wore had a high waist which concealed the tiny mound of her stomach.

Rebecca knew people would soon figure out the baby was conceived before the wedding, but there was nothing she could do about it. She had raised her son the right way, and was not responsible for the choices he made in life.

Remy walked into the kitchen whistling.

Rebecca hadn't seen him so excited about something in a long time. It made her happy to see him smiling.

"It's time for us to head to the church."

They left the kitchen.

Rebecca picked up a small box sitting near her purse in the dining room. "Megan, I have something for you. These pearls... they belonged to Remy's grandmother Gemma. They have been in the Tousssaint family since the 1700's. King Renaud II in France is said to have given them to his many great-grandmother Elyse. These are my gift to you—to welcome you into our family."

Megan's eyes filled with tears. "Thank you so much, Mrs. Toussaint. I can't begin to tell you what this means to me. I will cherish them forever." Placing her hand to her stomach, she said, "If this baby is a girl, she will one day wear them on her wedding day."

Rebecca nodded in approval. "It's our legacy."

Remy worked hard while Megan stayed at home with his mother. Rebecca taught her how to cook and clean properly. He knew his wife had lived a pampered life, but had no idea that she never had to lift a finger to do anything growing up. She even had a nanny to care for her.

Megan had taken to attending church with his mother on Sunday. She even went to Bible Study every now and then when she felt up to it. A couple of times, Remy had caught her praying. He hoped she wouldn't become a religious fanatic like his mother.

After she had the baby, Megan seemed to draw men to her like a magnet.

Remy never considered himself the jealous type, but her flirtatious behavior brought out the worse in him.

"You should be home with our son," he told her one night when she wanted to go to a party.

"It's Mardi Gras. Let's go out and have some fun," she pleaded. "All you do is work. I'm home stuck with the baby…"

"You're his mother," Remy responded. He considered the matter settled.

When the baby turned six months old, Megan's mother showed up at the house. She wanted her daughter to come home.

"Megan's not going anywhere," he told his

mother-in-law.

Her mother ignored him. "Honey, we really want you to come home. You can go back to school."

"I said my wife isn't going anywhere."

"Remy..." Rebecca said. "Let's hear her out."

"I don't need to hear anything. I can take care of my family."

"Megan, can we speak alone?" her mother asked.

Remy eyed his wife, who nodded.

"Megan..."

"I want to talk to my mother, Remy."

Rebecca took him by the arm. "C'mon son."

"Can you believe that woman?" he uttered.

Rebecca tried to calm him. "Son, this attitude of yours won't get you anywhere. Megan's a grown woman. If she wants to stay—she will. If not, then I say good riddance."

"And what about my son? Maurice isn't going anywhere with that bigot."

Minutes later, Megan called them back into the room.

"Remy, I love you and Maurice, but I want

to go home," she announced. "I want to go back to school. I can't just sit around here raising a child. I want something more out of life."

"So what are you saying?"

"I'm going home with my mother. I don't belong in this world."

Remy released a string of profanity.

Rebecca sent up prayers.

When he calmed down, he said, "My son isn't going anywhere."

Megan surprised him when she responded, "It's better that he stays with you, Remy."

He wanted to reach out and shake some sense into her, but restrained himself. "Get out of this house and don't you ever think about coming back."

Two years later, Remy married a nice church girl named Alice. She was great with Maurice.

One night he came to Rebecca and said, "Mama, I'm tired of running. I know what God wants me to do and I've been trying to ignore it for most of my life."

"What is it, son?"

"He want me to preach. I know it, Mama."

Tears rolled down Rebecca's cheeks. "Thank you, Lord. Thank you for not giving up on my boy."

Remy's eyes grew wet. "Pray with me, Mama."

They prayed for what seemed like half an hour, he wasn't sure how long, but when they finished—Remy felt as lighter than he had in years.

When Alice came home from work, she found them in the kitchen celebrating.

"Your husband's finally answering his true calling. He's going to preach."

"Honey, I'm so happy for you."

He kissed her. "I'm going to see Reverend Massey tomorrow."

"Do you want me to go with you?" she asked.

Remy shook his head. "No. It's something I need to do alone. Just pray for me."

Alice smiled. "I always do, my love." Taking his hand in hers, she said, "Since we're celebrating, this is the perfect time to tell you both that our family is about to grow."

Rebecca squealed with delight while Remy

picked up his wife and twirled her around.

Chapter 18

"Remy never heard from Megan again, from the looks of it." Myra said. "Granny once told me that she married some white politician in Mississippi. Now, you would've thought that Daddy would've learned from his father's mistake in marrying a white girl whose parents didn't approve of mixed marriages, but no… Maurice Toussaint was determined to do as he pleased. Well, we both know where that road took him."

Despite his father and stepmother's protests, Maurice up and married a white girl from Georgia. He went with his band to play at a club in Atlanta. Met Daisy Walters, fell in love and announced that they planned to marry after a few months.

Rebecca helped with the planning of the small ceremony and did her best to support the couple, but deep down, she was heartbroken about her grandson's choice. She did not want a repeat of what happened with Remy this time around.

Maurice's wedding day arrived.

Daisy was a beautiful bride. She wore a tailored cream suit with a hat that she designed herself with the Toussaint pearls.

Rebecca was tearful throughout the ceremony while Remy was sullen. He kept his emotions in check though while conducting the service.

"I'm so happy, Grandma," Maurice whispered in Rebecca's ear during the reception back at the house. "I love Daisy so much."

She touched his cheek. "If you're happy, so am I."

Rebecca watched them together during the reception. It was obvious to everyone around that Maurice was very much in love with Daisy.

"You can't deny that they look very happy together," she told her son.

Remy nodded in agreement. "That's what worries me, Mama. Megan and I had that same look on our wedding day. None of her family members came—this scene is an all too familiar one."

"Perhaps this one will end differently," Rebecca said. "Daisy is a wonderful cook and that woman can sew. She didn't grow up with a silver spoon in her mouth."

"From what I understand, her family isn't exactly poor either," Remy responded.

"Son, all we can do at this point is hope for the very best."

Two weeks had passed since Eleanor fell into the coma.

Myra jumped at the sound of someone entering the hospital room. She glanced over her shoulder in time to see Belva. "You nearly scared me to death," she told her. "I don't know why I'm so jumpy today."

"Probably because you're exhausted," her granddaughter responded.

Belva held out the bag she was holding in

her hand. "I brought an iPod and some portable speakers for Eleanor. I downloaded the *Bible Experience* on it. You can play it for her while you take a break from reading, or if you just want to take a nap."

Myra smiled. "Thank you, sugar. We will both listen to the word of God. I really enjoyed what I heard so far. I'ma have to get me one of those iPods."

"Nana, I'll let you have that one if you promise to take it easy. I want you to sit down in that chair and take a nap. I'll sit here with Eleanor until you wake up."

She was too tired to argue. "You sure you don't mind," Myra asked.

Belva shook his head. "I'll stay right here."

"Don't let me sleep too long," she told her.

"You will sleep as long as your body needs," Belva responded.

Myra decided to do as her granddaughter requested without further comment. She fell asleep as soon as she settled in the reclining chair.

When she opened her eyes, two hours had passed. Belva was sitting on the edge of the hospital bed, talking to Eleanor as she held her hand.

"You're awake."

She nodded and smiled. "I can't believe I slept so long."

"You were tired," she commented.

Myra rose slowly to her feet, her joints aching in protest. "I'm going to the bathroom, but I'll be right back."

Belva gave a slight nod.

"You were right, Belva," Myra stated when she came out. "I really needed that nap. I'm ready to take over from here."

"I was just telling Eleanor about the wedding and how I hope that she"ll be there."

Myra smiled. "Did you hear that, sister? You got to wake up so you can come to Belva's wedding. I can tell you—it's gonna be a fancy shindig."

Chapter 19

October 1950

Eleanor glanced over her shoulder, see-ing Ziraili in the back row.

She found herself sitting in a pew at her grandfather's church, wearing a black suit and tie. This time she was in the body of her father, Maurice Toussaint. When Eleanor glanced back over her shoulder, Ziraili had disappeared.

"Maurice, come on up here and grace us with a hymn," his father requested.

The little church was too small to hold the amount of people in attendance, so there were people everywhere, piled in pews, standing around the church and outside the building.

Maurice got up and walked over to the piano and began to play as he sang, *Amazing Grace,* his grandmother's favorite song. His eyes traveled to his wife Daisy, who sat next to Rebecca. She held their daughter, Eleanor in her arms.

As he returned to his seat, Maurice caught sight of a young woman staring at him. She cut her eyes toward Daisy and sent a scowl in his direction. It was clear she didn't approve of him marrying a white girl.

Maurice didn't care what she or anyone else thought when it came to Daisy. He loved her and that's all that mattered. Things were good between them on a personal level. Being married to a black man was causing Daisy some difficulty in getting sewing jobs at the more expensive shops, but she wasn't one to give up so easily. She decided she would just open up her own store.

In another month, her business would open, thanks in part to his grandmother and father. Maurice appreciated their help and vowed to pay them back as soon as they were able to do so.

At the end of service, Maurice took Daisy

and a sleeping Eleanor home. He sat at the piano playing softly while Daisy prepared something for them to eat.

"Babe, come here."

"You need something?" she asked.

Maurice pulled her down to sit on his lap. "Do you miss your family?"

"Not really," she responded.

He had a feeling she wasn't telling him the truth. "It's okay if you do," he said. "I know it's hard on you… the choice you made."

"This world is changing," Daisy said. "People are just gonna have to change with it."

He kissed her. "I suppose you're right, babe."

"Dr. King is gonna do it," she said. "I've been reading a lot of what he's been saying and he's right… racial segregation needs to end. I don't want Eleanor growing up in a world like this."

Maurice broke into a grin. "I've been thinking of joining the N.A.A.C.P."

"I think you should," Daisy responded. "There is strength in numbers, honey. "But be careful. I read some people attending a meeting got threatened by the KKK in Mississippi."

He nodded. "I heard 'bout that. It's a shame, but I'm not worried. I got the Lord on my side.

"Those folks probably said the same thing."

Rising to her feet, she said, "I need to see to dinner. You keep playing that pretty song."

The more Maurice thought about what was going on in places like Georgia and Mississippi, the more he wanted to get involved.

He considered his family history. His lineage could be traced to Africa, France and even Scotland.

It was time for people to look beyond skin color.

"I think that's everything," Julia said. "The wedding is planned and we've ordered everything but the invitations."

Belva smiled. "We have plenty of time for those."

Myra brought in a plate of sandwiches. "I hope you're all hungry."

"I am," Julia stated.

"Me, too," Belva said.

The hospital called.

Myra answered the phone. She hung up a few minutes later, saying, "I need to go.

Winston's trying to have Eleanor moved to a long-term care facility. I'm not gonna let that happen."

"Maybe it's for the best," Julia responded.

"I want to talk to the doctor."

Myra drove to the hospital as quickly as she could without getting a speeding ticket. When she arrived, she found Winston in the room with Eleanor.

"She's not going anywhere," Myra stated.

"You don't have any say in this matter."

"Give her a chance, Winston."

He winced at her mention of him by his first name, but Myra wasn't about to back down or cower in his presence.

"Eleanor is going to come through this."

"She may have some brain damage. What then?"

"We will cross that bridge when it comes," she responded. "I'm not even considering the worse. I believe in divine healing and I fully expect my God to come through for Eleanor and my granddaughter."

"I'm not trying to punish my wife for deceiving me," Winston stated. "I know that's what you think."

"But you feel differently about her?"

He looked Myra straight in the face. "I love Eleanor. That hasn't changed."

"Then why are you cheating on her?" she asked.

"I don't know if I can answer that. It's complicated."

"You don't have to tell me the reason—you are going to have to explain that to your wife when she wakes up."

"You're going to tell her about—"

"That D.A. tramp..." Myra interjected. "No, I'm not, but do you really think Eleanor doesn't know that you're cheating on her? She's always been a smart girl."

Winston suddenly looked uncomfortable.

"If you really care about Eleanor, then visit with her... talk to her. She needs to hear your voice."

"I... I can't."

He left the room before Myra could respond.

***

"When you're young, you have the impression that you're going to live forever. At least, that's what I used to think."

Myra released a soft chuckle as she brushed the hair away from Eleanor's forehead. "When I was a teenager, I thought I knew everything. Humph! Nobody could tell me anything. I bet you were probably the very same way."

Reflecting back over her youth, Myra could almost smell the sweet peachy scent of her grandmother's cobbler.

"I sure wish granny was still alive. I miss her so much. Alice may not have been our dad's biological mother, but she loved him and she took good care of me."

Myra began to sing softly as she stroked Eleanor's cheek.

She released a long sigh. "Honey, wake up. Eleanor, you and I have so much to talk about."

A tear slipped from her eye.

Myra dropped down into the chair beside the bed, her hands propped under her chin. "Lord, please wake my sister. Please save her."

Chapter 20

After the death of his father in 1952, Maurice lost his job after showing up drunk more than once, so he began taking small gigs with his former band.

"What's going on with you?" Daisy asked. "You've been drinking a lot lately. Especially since you started hanging with Chuck and the fellas. You a married man."

"Woman, I'm just out there having a good time."

"You had such a time of it that you lost your job. Did you think I wouldn't find out?"

Maurice looked at her. "I'm a musician."

Daisy nodded. "But do you have to be a drunk musician?" She took his hand and placed it over her stomach. "We're going to have another baby soon."

He was not happy. "How could you let this happen? We're struggling with one mouth to feed. That shop of yours isn't doing that well, let you tell it."

She walked over to a nearby window. "I didn't get this way all by myself."

Maurice followed her. "I'm sorry. You know I'm doing everything I can for my family. Another baby..."

She faced him. "Then stop all the drinking and get a real job. All this running around with your friends—you hardly bring any money home."

Drinking wasn't the only thing Maurice had been into—he was also experimenting with drugs.

Two days later, he broke into a shop downtown and stole five hundred dollars. The band had a gig in Georgia and had come to him for money. Instead of going to his grandmother, Maurice decided to steal it.

Daisy didn't care for his friends and he didn't

want to hear her complain about his frequent road trips, so Maurice stole away in the middle of the night. He felt a thread of guilt running off like this and leaving Daisy home alone. He knew that she really missed her family.

She had written them to tell them of her marriage and of Eleanor's birth. She had yet to receive a response.

Two days later, when Maurice returned, he was met by an angry Daisy.

"Did you do it?" she demanded. "Did you break into my shop?"

"Leave me alone, woman," he shouted. "I'm a man. I don't have to tell you nothing. Besides you been lying to me about how much money the shop is making."

Daisy placed her hand on her hips and said, "I'm not gonna let you take every penny we make and spend it on liquor and whatever else."

"That money is just as much mine as it is yours," Maurice uttered. "It's the Toussaint money that put you in that store. *My* family did that."

She stormed off into the bedroom, slamming the door behind her.

***

The next morning, Maurice was apologetic.

"I'm sorry for what I did," he told her over breakfast.

"I'm worried 'bout all the drinking you been doing."

"Don't be," he interjected. "I'm just having some fun. I got everything under control. I can handle my liquor."

"I never knew that you drank like that," Daisy stated. "I've only seen you drink a beer every now and then before your daddy died. When you started hanging with that band… now you tossing back everything from rum to brandy."

"I'm a grown man, baby."

She pushed away from the table and rose to her feet. "I need to get out of here. I'm having a safe installed at the shop."

When Daisy returned that evening, she found Maurice waiting on her. When he pulled her into his arms, she could smell the alcohol on his breath and turned up her nose.

She turned her face away from him. She

loved Maurice more than anything, but she hated whenever he was drunk, high or both.

"Why you turning away from me?" he asked, slurring the words.

"You know I don't like the smell of alcohol. It stinks."

Maurice rose to his feet muttering a string of curses. "I don't know who you think you are… telling me my breath stink… your breath ain't all minty fresh either."

"You're doing more than just drinking, aren't you?" She asked.

He shrugged in nonchalance. "It's not a big deal."

"Are you addicted to cocaine?"

Maurice looked surprised. "Who you been talking to?"

"Betty came to see me today."

Maurice made a mental note to tell his drummer to keep his girlfriend in check. She had no right going to Daisy and running her mouth.

"It's just for fun and to feel good."

"That's where all your money is going," Daisy said. "I don't want this around my children, Maurice. You need to leave."

"*Leave.* Woman, this is my house."

"If you won't leave, then I will," Daisy said, standing her ground.

He laughed. "You ain't got nowhere to go. Your own family don't want you now that you've been with a black man."

Maurice's words cut deeper than he ever could have imagined.

Daisy moved in with his grandmother.

For the first couple of weeks, he tried to coax her back home, but she refused.

Over the course of their separation, Maurice came to her a few times, asking for money. He was nice initially, but then tried to bully her.

Daisy threatened to call the police.

"You would do that to your own husband?"

She wiped away her tears. "Maurice, you need help. Miss Rebecca said she—"

He interrupted her by saying, "You told my grandmother my business." He was angry.

"Baby, we all love you. We just want you to get well."

Maurice shook his head. "Naw. That ain't love. That's control."

He walked toward the front door. "I'm outta here."

"I can't keep doing this with you, Maurice."

He stopped in his tracks. "Doing what? Telling people my business?"

"Baby, you need help."

"I came here just to get a few dollars. That's the help I need, Daisy."

She wiped away her tears. "I'm not going to give you money to buy drugs. I'm sorry, but I won't do that."

The doctor came in to check on Eleanor shortly after eleven o'clock.

"How's she doing this morning?" he asked.

"I wish I could tell you that she's awake," Myra said. "I'm not giving up on her though."

While he examined Eleanor, she used that time to relieve her bladder in the bathroom.

When Myra came out, he was gone. She and the nurse talked briefly.

There was still no change.

"I know she gonna get better. This is her wilderness, but God is gonna bring her out. I believe that. Delayed don't mean denied."

"Amen to that, Miss Myra. You've been a really good sister. You've hardly left this hospital."

"I don't like leaving Eleanor," she confessed. "I need to be here when she wakes up. I know that most people don't understand this, but it's important that I be the first face she sees."

"Why don't we send up a prayer just thanking God for all he's about to do in your sister's life?"

Myra smiled. "I'd like that."

They held hands while the nurse prayed. Myra reached over and covered her Eleanor's hand with her own.

When the nurse left, Myra was in high spirits.

Chapter 21

"Who is this fool?" Maurice demanded in a loud voice.

"This is Reverend James," Daisy said. "Miss Rebecca thought it would be good if the pastor came over here to talk to us."

Maurice started at him from head to toe. "He sho' don't look like no preacher I know. What you doing here, preacher?"

His mouth tightened, but instead of responding, Reverend James ignored him.

"Ain't nothing here for you, pastor. I don't need your help or your sermons or your prayers."

"Your family loves you, but you're right about not needing me or sermons. You need God. As for prayer, it never hurts."

Maurice launched into a cussing session at Reverend James, which only served to make Daisy feel worse.

"If you need help, Sister, you know where we are," the minster stated before walking away.

"Why you do that?" Daisy asked. "You didn't have to be so mean to Reverend James. He and his wife have been real nice to me and here you are acting stupid."

"Shut up, woman," he uttered.

"You shut up," Daisy countered before turning her back on him. "This is not the way my life was supposed to go. We had so many wonderful dreams for our life together, and you've just tossed it all away. What hurts most is that I chose *you* over my own family."

"Daisy…"

She shook her head. "I can't do this anymore. I found a place for me and the kids. Maurice, I'm going to file for divorce after the baby's born."

He was speechless. He'd never really believed that she would leave him, but now it seemed that Daisy wasn't coming back.

"I can change," he said. "I promise I'll do better. I'll get the help... whatever you want me to do."

"I want you to want to get better for yourself."

Later that evening, Maurice sought out Reverend James.

The man didn't bother to disguise his surprise. "What an awesome God we serve. I surely didn't expect to see you this soon."

"Sir, I apologize for earlier." Maurice's eyes teared up. "I can't lose my family. I need you to help me."

The next night, Maurice burst into the shop. He had never been so scared. He'd spent the evening before with the pastor, talking and praying.

For the first time in a long time, he felt hopeful, but that was short-lived. His past was coming back to haunt him.

"Daisy, we got to get out of here right now," he told her.

"What's going on?" she asked him, her heart racing. "Maurice, what did you do?"

"I owe this crazy dude a lot of money. If I don't give it to them tonight—Daisy, he gon kill me." He began to cry.

"How much money do you owe?"

"Over two thousand," Maurice responded.

"I only have half of that in the safe."

"Where are the pearls?" he asked. "I know they worth a lot of money."

Daisy gasped. "They've been in your family for years, Maurice. I can't do that to your grandmother."

"Do you want me to die?" He demanded. "I thought you loved me."

"I'll go with you to find these people. Maybe we can give them the thousand and work out a payment plan or something. We'll ask them for more time."

"Myra, it don't work like that. These guys— they mean what they say. They'll kill me for sure."

Convinced that giving them half the money would buy them time, a pregnant Daisy accompanied Maurice to the vacant building where a group of men were gathered.

He asked to see a man called Treble.

They are taken to a dark alley where a lone man wearing a black patch over one eye stood leaning against a fence in desperate need of painting.

Maurice was visibly trembling, and so was Daisy.

He handed the money to the one-eyed evil looking man.

"I'll get you the other half. I just need some time," Daisy told him.

"Time's up," he said, pulling out a gun.

"Please sir," she begged. "Just give us a chance to get the money."

"Your man been stealing my drugs. I can't let him get away with that."

"Sir, if you would give me a chance, I'll get the money. *I will.*"

Maurice suddenly backed away, then turned and sprinted into a run.

Shots rang out.

Daisy screamed.

He fell to his knees as his light brown jacket turned red.

When she reached him, Maurice had tears in his eyes and he was trying to talk. "S-sorr-y…"

He pointed.

Daisy cowered in fear as the drug lord approached.

Maurice kept trying to speak. He wanted his wife to know that she and the baby would be fine. The woman standing behind Treble had told him so. He had heard the stories over the years and knew who she was.

"Zi… Ziraili…" he managed to get out. "H-here."

Daisy closed her eyes and prayed in earnest. She could hear Maurice murmuring something over and over, but she couldn't focus on his words in all the chaos around them. She felt his body go slack and knew he was gone.

Treble stuck the gun in her mouth and pulled the trigger.

In shock, Daisy's eyes flew open.

Treble pulled the gun out of her mouth, pointed it at her face, and pulled the trigger a second time.

He appeared shaken by what happened as much as Daisy was.

Treble checked the gun and pointed it at her.

The gun still refused to fire.

"I guess your God has his arms all around you, cracker. Don't let me ever see you again and if you tell anyone what happened—I will kill you."

Daisy got up and rushed away, not once looking back. She ran out of the alley as fast as her swollen belly would allow. She wouldn't go back to her apartment because she was scared to death that Treble would follow her or have some of his men come after her.

She stepped on the first bus that arrived, heading anywhere.

Daisy couldn't shake the image of seeing her husband shot and killed right before her eyes. The memory of this night would forever be imprinted on her brain. She kept her head down and wiped away her tears. She was still shaking and her heart still beat at a rapid pace.

She got off the bus in a relatively safe part of town and made her way to the train station.

Daisy went into the bathroom and hid in one of the stalls. There she cried for Maurice. She loved him dearly and his loss was unbearable. Now she was alone and scared. She had no money except for a few dollars; she was pregnant—Daisy didn't know what to do.

She groaned as a strong contraction hit followed by a gush of liquid. The baby was coming, and there was no one around to help her.

Daisy prayed as she strained involuntarily to expel the child from her body. Panting, she managed to remove her underwear.

She was too weak to stand, so she sat down on the floor.

Another contraction forced a loud moan.

She heard someone enter the bathroom. "Help me, please."

A black woman opened the door to the stall. "Lawdy, Miss… you about to have that baby."

From the way she was dressed, Daisy could tell she had come in to clean the bathroom. "Save my baby," she whispered.

Working quickly, the woman made a pallet using Daisy's coat for her to lay down. "You gon' be fine, Miss. My name's Waverly. I helped my sister deliver my niece and nephew into this world. I know just what to do. Is your husband here?"

Daisy shook her head. "He's dead."

Waverly stared at the blood on her dress, but said nothing.

Two contractions later, Daisy felt the unmistakable urge to push.

With yet another push, a minute or so later, Daisy could feel the baby's head crowning.

"You doing real good, Miss."

One more huge contraction and Daisy felt her baby leave her body.

"It's a precious lil' girl," Waverly announced. She wrapped the baby in a cloth towel.

The baby started to cry.

I have another daughter.

Daisy laid the little girl over her knees with her head lower than her bottom, remembering that from some section of a pregnancy book she had read during a previous pregnancy. It was supposed to help drain the fluid from the nose and mouth.

Daisy searched her memory, trying to remember if there was anything else she should do. She knew it was most important to keep the infant warm.

Waverly removed a pocketknife from her bag and was about to cut the umbilical cord when another contraction hit Daisy.

The urge to push was overwhelming.

She delivered the placenta.

Weak from the delivery of her daughter, Daisy lay there, her eyes closed as Waverly cleaned her up. "I'ma go get some help."

"Call Rebecca Toussaint," she told the woman. "Tell her to meet me at the hospital."

The door to the bathroom opened and closed.

An hour later, Daisy was in her hospital room with a grieving Rebecca by her side. They were joined shortly after by Alice Toussaint, Maurice's stepmother.

"Why didn't you come to me?" Rebecca said. "I would've given you the money."

"He didn't want you to know." Daisy started to cry. "This is my fault. I should've given him the pearls when he asked for them."

"No, you shouldn't have," Alice uttered. "That necklace is priceless. I loved Maurice like my own, but he's the only one to blame in this. I told that boy to leave them drugs alone."

"She doesn't need to hear this right now," Rebecca stated. "Regardless of his choices, Maurice didn't deserve to die like he did."

"Why didn't this… this thug shoot you?" Alice questioned. "I'm surprised he'd leave you alive, knowing you can identify him."

"He tried," Daisy said. "More than once, but the gun wouldn't fire."

Rebecca stretched her arms upward. "Thank you Father for protecting Daisy and the baby. Thank you."

Daisy wiped her tears with the back of her hand. "He threatened to kill me if I went to the police or even told anyone. I'm scared."

"It might be a good idea for you and the children to leave town," Alice said. "I'll call my sister Eunice. She lives in Chicago."

"Thank you, Miss Alice."

"I'll go to your place and pack some clothes for you and Eleanor."

"Where is my little girl?"

"I left her with Sadie," Rebecca said, referring to her housekeeper.

"Before Maurice died, he kept trying to tell me something." Daisy shook her head. "I felt like it was important, but I couldn't understand him. It was like he was saying something foreign."

Rebecca sat down on the edge of her bed. "Was it a name?"

Daisy shrugged. "I don't know."

"Did it sound like Ziraili?" Alice asked.

"I think that was it?" Daisy looked at her. "What is it?"

"You need to rest," Rebecca interjected. "You've been through a terrible ordeal."

A week later, Daisy boarded a train bound for Chicago.

Maurice's body was found in a swamp the following week. The police never knew his wife had witnessed his murder. They were told that she was on her way out of town when she went into labor, which is why she was at the train station. It was assumed that her trip to Chicago had been delayed by the birth of her child.

Myra decided to get rid of some stuff that had been packed away for years. She sat a box of her late husband's clothes near the door. She would have Julia take them down to the church. Maybe they could be of some use to someone else.

She found a box of her great-grandmother's belongings. Granny had told her once that Rebecca Toussaint was the type of woman to hang onto everything. She never liked giving or throwing anything away.

She opened the box.

It contained photographs, legal documents and other memorabilia.

Myra went through them one by one. She stopped cold when she saw her mother's death certificate.

Chapter 22

Daisy and the children returned to New Orleans after Treble had been killed in a shootout with the police over the murder of an unidentified man found dead in an alley.

Rebecca silently noted that she was not the same girl who'd left four months earlier. She imagined that Daisy had relieved the horror of what happened to Maurice almost every single night.

Alice and Rebecca had kept the store opened for her.

Daisy tried to stay busy, working from morning until hours after the store closed.

"That girl too afraid to be alone with her thoughts," Alice told her mother-in-law.

Rebecca agreed. "She rarely leaves the house when she's not working."

That evening, when Daisy came home, Alice said, "It's not healthy for you to stay locked up in here like this. You need to get out and socialize with people your own age."

"I'm scared all the time," Daisy confessed. "I've had to deal with so much…" she shook her head. "I'm not ready."

Rebecca and Alice left her alone.

They had no idea how much Daisy missed her parents, and wished she could go back home, but too much had happened.

She was traveling in a downward spiral of depression.

A lone tear escaped Eleanor's eye.

Myra bent over and wiped it away with her finger. "Honey, if you can hear me, please don't give up," she whispered. "Eleanor, you have a family who loves you beyond measure.

Open your eyes. C'mon sugar… just open

those beautiful blue eyes of yours."

Myra wiped away her own tears with the back of her hand.

"Eleanor, I love you. I have always loved you. I want you to know that." She released a long sigh. "To tell you the truth, I would give just about anything for you to wake up. Even the Tussaint pearls. You mean more to me than that necklace."

Myra rose to her feet. "I don't know what you're thinking, but you can't leave this world until God is ready for you to go. Believe me, I know. He allowed our daddy to be killed, but He spared mine and Mama's life. He wouldn't let that man kill her that night."

She walked over to the window. "Mama, she never was quite right after that. I guess you know this better than me, since you were the oldest... I always thought someone had come to the house and killed her. I thought they kidnapped you. It never occurred to me that you'd run away."

Myra glanced over her shoulder. "I found Mama's death certificate in Granny's things a few days ago. She killed herself."

She returned to Eleanor's side. "Did you

know this? Is that why you ran away?"

"Ziraili, I've seen enough. I want to go home."

"This is where you have to face the past."

"I know what happened," Eleanor said. "I lived it."

"You blame your father for what happened."

"My mother was so afraid. She jumped at just about anything. I was afraid because she was so scared."

"She didn't know you where home that day."

Eleanor looked at Ziraili. "I was picked to be in the school play. I was so excited and couldn't wait to tell her. Myra was playing around, so I left her and ran all the way home. I walked into the house and went to her bedroom... I saw her just as the gun went off."

She shivered in the darkness. "I saw the pearls on the dresser. I took them and ran as fast as I could. I went to the train station. I sat there sobbing my eyes out. This woman, she came over and wanted to know if I was okay. I lied and said I'd lost my ticket home. She was kind and offered to purchase another for me. That's how I ended up in Baton Rouge."

No one suspected the truth.

Eleanor caught sight of herself in the window of Antoinette's as she listened to Twyla Hartwood's endless chatter.

Feeling the swirling heat surround her, Eleanor was thankful for the wide hat that shielded her from the August sun. While Twyla talked on and on about the upcoming party, Eleanor glanced around her, admiring the grandiose beauty of the southern part of Baton Rouge.

Eleanor opened the door to the dress shop and was about to enter when a gush of wind whipped around her as a woman of medium height breezed into the shop in front of them.

Glancing over at Twyla, she wore a stunned expression. "Who is that? Why, she acts as if she owns the place."

The woman had the look of old money—wide, high cheekbones, a serene, direct blue-eyed gaze. Beneath her fashionable hat, she wore her blonde hair in an aristocratic pompa-dour.

Before Twyla could reply, she stopped sud-denly and turned to face them.

"I've seen you around, but we haven't been formally introduced," she addressed Eleanor in a voice laced with the sweetness of the South.

"Mrs. Blakemore," Twyla interjected cheer-fully. "This is Eleanor Toussaint. She and I at-tend school together."

Eleanor's mouth opened but no sound came out. Standing before her was the weal-thiest woman in Baton Rouge. The Blakemo-re family was one of the richest families in the world, having made millions in the railroad business. Owning a railroad was not enough, however. The Blakemore family had an entire small-gauge steam railroad with four chugging locomotives on their vast acreage of land.

Mrs. Blakemore removed her gloves as she scrutinized Eleanor. Her expression, one of snobbery. "I'm Mrs. Winston Fitzgerald Blakemore II. It's lovely to meet you, dear. I trust you'll be attending the party with Twyla." It was a statement and not a question.

Finding her voice, Eleanor managed to say,

"Mrs. Blakemore, it's very nice to meet you. Thank you for including me in the celebration."

She smiled. "The Hartwoods' are dear friends of ours. I would be remiss if I didn't invite their special guest. I detect a Southern accent. Where are you from, dear?"

"Eleanor's from New Orleans," Twyla announced. "Her grandfather was of French noble birth, you know."

"Really?"

A saleslady approached the three women, cutting off the question that was surely on Mildred Blakemore's lips. Ignoring Eleanor and Twyla, she asked, "Mrs. Blakemore, what can I do for you?"

As they walked away, Eleanor leaned over and whispered, "What a frightful woman."

Twyla giggled. "Don't worry about Mrs. Blakemore. She's absolutely harmless."

Eleanor wasn't so sure, but she kept her musings to herself. As Mrs. Blakemore talked, she noticed the way she gestured with her hands. Her mannerisms were those of a boarding school graduate.

"...As you may have heard, I'm giving a party in honor of my son's birthday. It's going to be a grand affair and I'm looking for a very special gown. Agnes tells me that you have some new selections from Paris ..." Mrs. Blakemore ran her hands across a mauve silk moiré fabric. "This is exquisite."

Eleanor stood quietly beside Twyla, watching Mrs. Blakemore in fascination. She moved slowly around the shop pretending to inspect the rows and rows of dresses in an array of colors and fabrics. When she looked up, she found Mildred Blakemore observing her as well.

Mrs. Blakemore awarded her with a quick, insincere smile, and then turned when someone called out to her.

"Why Mildred, it's so good to see you. Jane and I are looking forward to the ball. As a matter of fact, that's why we're here. We're picking up our gowns today."

Twyla nudged Eleanor. "Here, I think you'd look beautiful in these." She handed her two dresses.

Eleanor held up one gown and smiled. It was made of silk and embellished with beads and lots of heirloom lace. The dress was beautiful and the bright color was perfect for evening but the second dress was not to her liking, so she discarded it. Attending the Blakemore party would be an interesting experience, and Eleanor could barely contain her excitement. She had never been to such a fancy party before.

Watching Mrs. Blakemore, she smiled inwardly. If she only knew ...

Twyla nudged her gently and whispered, "See that woman talking to Mrs. Blakemore?"

When Eleanor nodded, she continued, "That's Ida Oppenheimer, and that's her daughter, Jane, standing beside her. Plain Jane, I call her. Mrs. Oppenheimer's hoping Jane and Winston will marry."

"I see. I wonder how he feels about it?"

Twyla shrugged. "Jane's marriage to Winston would only be a business deal. Knowing him as I do, I don't think he'll just sit back and let his parents dictate whom he'll marry. He's not the type."

Eleanor eyed her friend. "You seem to know him pretty well."

"Our families are old friends. I can't wait for the two of you to meet."

"So you keep telling me. Why is that?"

"You'll see," Twyla responded cryptically, leaving Eleanor to wonder what her friend had in mind.

Chapter 23

Eleanor said goodnight to Twyla and headed to the bedroom next door. She loved the room in which she'd been staying for the last couple of weeks. The guest room had been tastefully decorated in the latest fashion. The striped silk cushions were a pale pink accented by a darker pink on the chairs and the gold-fringed draperies added a bold contrast to the softness of the bedcovers. The understated richness of the room put the opulence of her family home in New Orleans to shame.

She sat in front of the mirror, staring at her complexion as she removed the pins from her soft brown mane. Shaking her head, she released the curly mass. A prominent dark mole above her lips accented her large, blue eyes and set off her soft, unlined ivory skin. Her thick hair had a natural curl and she never took much time with it. Eleanor's complexion was as light as that of an average white person.

Although she looked white, with honey-colored hair, thin lips and nose—it was that drop of colored blood that tainted her. Being colored meant she didn't have the right to live the same life as the whites. But it was by their law that she couldn't, and Eleanor resented it. She was of mixed race and strongly believed it should be her choice as to how she lived her life.

Eleanor wasn't after money. None of the teachers or students ever knew of her colored blood. To them, she was as white as they were.

Seeing the former Toussaint estate in New Orleans for the first time when she was eight years old, was an awakening experience for Eleanor. It was a glimpse into the insulated, pampered life that having white skin could penetrate.

Eleanor remembered standing outside the

massive iron gates surrounding the vast estate and asking her mother why they didn't live there. Daisy's voice was sad as she responded, "You are not yet old enough to understand."

Now, twelve years later, Eleanor truly understood.

When it came to Twyla, she felt a moment's guilt for deceiving her dearest friend. She'd often wondered how Twyla would react if she knew that her closest friend was colored.

Twyla and her beau, Stuart Hamilton was out riding and planned to have a picnic by the lake on the Hartwood property. Eleanor had been invited, but feeling the couple wanted some time alone, she'd politely turned them down.

Alone, she decided to tour the Hartwood Estate. Outside, Eleanor strolled to the carriage house that sat directly to the rear of the stables. There, she found Jonah, the Hartwood's colored chauffeur.

Smiling brightly, she called out, "Good afternoon, Jonah."

"Miz Toussaint, good afternoon, ma'am. Somewhere I can take you?"

"No, Jonah. Thank you but I'm just taking a stroll. The grounds are so beautiful."

"Yes, ma'am. They sure is." He moved to leave. "Well, I's better gets back to work. Good day to you, ma'am."

Eleanor realized he never looked her directly in the eye, and knew he felt uncomfortable around her.

She knew the reason why.

Eleanor headed back to the huge three-story mansion that sat amidst the magnolia trees.

Climbing the steps, Eleanor headed into the tiled entrance and down the hallway. On the right lay the living room and a parlor with high-carved plaster ceilings.

Standing in the doorway of the parlor, Eleanor savored the feel of the intricately hand-carved mahogany woodwork. She determined one day to have a house as grand as this.

Hungry for something to read, she headed to the east side of the hallway and into the library. Scanning the shelves, Eleanor selected a book of English poetry to read.

Just as she was about to climb the large

staircase, a beaming Twyla returned home.

"Eleanor, I'm so glad to see you. I've got so much to tell you. Today is simply the best day of my life."

"Then come on, don't keep me waiting."

Together, like giggling schoolgirls, they headed up the stairs to Twyla's room.

As soon as Eleanor sank down beside Twyla on the bed, her friend announced, "Scott proposed. He's asked me to marry him and I accepted."

She reached over to hug Twyla. "I'm very happy for you."

"I'm so happy. I never thought he'd ask me this soon."

Eleanor smiled knowingly. "Well, it's obvious he's in love with you. Why, he looks just like a cute little puppy dog whenever you're around."

Twyla playfully pinched Eleanor's arm. "You're so mean. Scott doesn't look anything like a puppy dog. He's the most attractive man here in Baton Rouge."

"I thought you said Winston Blakemore was the most handsome," Eleanor teased.

"Well, he *is* handsome, but not like my

Scott. However, he does have the most money."

Eleanor smiled. "But money is not always important."

Twyla laughed. "And this coming from a woman born of privilege. Why, dear, you'd never trade places with someone born poor. I'm sure you'll agree that having money, and lots of it certainly has it's entitlements."

Eleanor did not respond. Twyla was right.

"... Scott's going to speak to my father tonight after dinner."

Eleanor snapped out of her musings. "I'm really happy for you, Twyla."

"Of course you'll stay until after the wedding, won't you?"

"I hadn't really anticipated staying here that long. I'm due in—"

"Atlanta's not going anywhere, dear Eleanor." She twisted her mouth into an unattractive frown. "I don't understand why you want to live there anyway. Why don't you just stay here? Don't you like Baton Rouge?"

"I love it here, but—"

Twyla was still pouting. "Then why won't you consider moving here?"

Smiling, Eleanor said, "I'll give it some

thought." The truth was that she'd hoped Twyla would invite her to stay on because she really didn't have anywhere else to go. After she arrived in Baton Rouge all those years ago, Eleanor went to a church for sanctuary. She was provided a home by one of the women in the parish.

When she met Twyla at a women's preparatory college, Eleanor gave her a sad story of how her parents had been killed while visiting family in France.

"It would be so wonderful having you here. Our children would grow up together, and our daughters—"

"Our children?" Eleanor interjected. "Why, I don't even have a beau."

Deep down, she was lonely but had to be very careful to whom she gave her heart. Because of who she was, the man she married would have to be a very special man indeed. He would have to understand the choices she'd made for herself, and any children she might have. With that in mind, Eleanor wondered if such a man existed.

***

"Eleanor, I think you're going to be the most exquisite creature at the party."

Smiling, she assessed herself in the full-length mirror. Her floor-length gown and simple train bespoke of French couture designer, Paul Poiret's influence. Eleanor could see Twyla's reflection in the mirror.

Twyla was not what one would consider beautiful, however, her pinched upper class white look could be construed as striking, Eleanor concluded. "You really are such a dear. I have to say… you look stunning."

Blushing, Twyla continued to talk non-stop. "I just know we're going to have such a wonderful time. The Blakemore parties are the best. Mrs. Blakemore told Mother that the Astors are coming. They're close friends of the Blakemores', you know."

Eleanor tried to swallow her nervousness.

"You look so scared, Eleanor," Twyla observed. "You needn't worry so. Why, I could scratch your eyes out. I'm so jealous of that flawless skin of yours. You don't wear any eye makeup or rouge and you're still so beautiful."

Eleanor only used cold cream at night and in the morning she rinsed it off. Then she would apply lipstick and the barest hint of powder. She recalled the many times her mother would say that she'd inherited the best features of both parents.

Chapter 24

Eleanor and Twyla arrived just behind the Milton's, a rich family from Mississippi. With the assistance of a man dressed in tails and top hat, a woman swathed in a gown made of satin and sparkling with jewels that spoke of their wealth stepped out of a gleaming Rolls Royce Silver Ghost.

Spotting them, the Milton's looked down their nose and gave an almost imperceptible nod in their direction.

Twyla and her parent's were clearly insulted.

Eleanor simply chose not to be offended.

Looking at the mansion, she was completely in awe.

Who in the world needed a place this big? she wondered.

Blakemore Manor. Four stories and approximately fifty-eight rooms, Twyla had proudly announced to her earlier.

The imposing entranceway sported a grand pediment and pillars that had been scrubbed clean for tonight's celebration. The brass fittings on the double doors gleamed in the moonlight.

Following Mr. and Mrs. Maynard Hartwood, Eleanor and Twyla entered an enormous foyer hung with ancestral portraits and tiled in a creamy Italian marble. Twyla pointed to a portrait and whispered that Mildred Blakemore's lineage went as far back as Sir Robert Manor, an English poet.

Eleanor was not impressed.

She, in fact, had never heard of him, but it was obvious to her that Mrs. Blakemore was very proud of her ancestors.

Eleanor walked through the long hallway, admiring the high ceilings and elegant rosewood chairs that sat against the soaring walls.

Mildred Blakemore greeted them in a syrupy voice. "I'm so glad you could join us. You, too, Eleanor, dear."

She forced a smile. "You have a lovely home, Mrs. Blakemore."

"How kind of you to say so. This house has been in the Blakemore family for generations."

Leading them to the ballroom, Mildred made small talk with Twyla's parents as they headed in the direction of the elder Winston Blakemore, leaving Eleanor and Twyla to survey and comment on the gowns worn by many of the guests garbed in the latest fashions.

"Look at that Jane," Twyla whispered. "That gown is simply not her color. She looks dreadful in pink. And those flowers in her hair are horrid. Why, she simply looks sickly."

Eleanor noticed that all of the waiters were men the color of soft caramel. She supposed that the Blakemore family only allowed colored men with light skin in their house. Seeing this, Eleanor felt perverse pleasure deep down that she was able to fool people who put so much stock in skin color.

Feeling the hair on the back of her neck stand up, Eleanor turned around.

Standing a few feet away, a tall man with

the prettiest eyes she'd ever seen was watching her. His teeth, even and white, contrasted pleasingly with his creamy skin. A swath of blond, wavy hair fell a little forward onto his forehead. Eleanor estimated him to be in his mid-twenties. Not wanting to appear too interested, she smiled politely before turning away.

Twyla nudged her gently. "Come on, I want to introduce you to Winston. Oh, here he comes now."

Eleanor glanced up in time to see the man she'd noticed just minutes earlier coming their way. His movements were swift, full of grace and virility.

"Twyla, it's good to see you," Winston said as he bent to kiss her cheek. Not once taking his eyes off of Eleanor, he said, "I'd heard you had a school chum visiting."

"Winston, dear, I'd like you to meet Eleanor Toussaint."

He grinned boyishly. "Eleanor, it's a pleasure to finally meet you. I've heard so much about you."

She smiled prettily. "It's very nice to meet you, too. And happy birthday, Mr. Blakemore."

"Please, call me Winston. You're among

friends."

Throughout Twyla and Winston's light bantering, Eleanor could barely take her eyes off him. His compelling eyes, his firm features, and the confident set of his shoulders fascinated her. Eleanor found herself studying his profile.

Trying not to get caught staring at Winston, she transferred her gaze to Twyla, who smiled in subtle amusement.

Dinner was announced and he escorted them into the spacious dining room.

They were seated and dinner was served, which consisted of clear soup, gigantic shrimp and oysters, venison, chicken, paper-thin slices of ham and four vegetables.

Eleanor found it hard to concentrate on her food. She could feel Winston's eyes on her. The man seated next to her kept trying to solicit a promise from her of a dance later.

Every now and then, she could feel Twyla kicking her softly and nodding in Jane Oppenheimer's direction. Eleanor stifled a laugh when Jane, eyeing Winston hungrily, almost missed placing her fork in her mouth.

Obviously embarrassed, Jane then picked up her glass of wine, only to spill some of it on her dress. Eleanor shifted her eyes to her plate when a flustered Mildred Blakemore glanced in her direction.

Across from her, Twyla was bursting at the seams, trying not to laugh out loud. Shaking her head, Eleanor resumed eating. When she chanced a look at

Winston, he, too, seemed to be bursting with silent laughter.

Eleanor needed some fresh air.

Easing away from the ballroom, she decided to take a stroll outside. The night air was still warm, and she wanted to take a peek at the much talked about Blakemore gardens.

There she saw rows upon rows of newly planted flowers and a mass of well-shaped rosebushes. Marble statues sparkled in the moonlight as if just washed, and the white pebble walkway that meandered through the garden was clear of all debris.

Eleanor loved flowers and adored roses especially. The rows of neat rosebushes were well maintained. She found roses of every imaginable color. Unable to resist the temptation, she leaned over to inhale the sweet fragrance of a pink rose.

"How do you like our garden?"

Eleanor jumped, clutching the silk bag she carried to her breast. "You nearly frightened me out of my wits." She took a deep breath, then another and another.

Winston stepped back. "I'm sorry. I didn't mean to scare you."

Smiling, Eleanor gestured around her. "You have a splendid garden. I love roses."

"As you can see, so does my mother."

With a shiver of vivid recollection, she said, "My grandmother had a rose garden back home. Of course it wasn't nearly as grand as this, but I loved it just the same."

"How long will you be staying here in Baton Rouge?"

"Until Twyla's wedding. Then I'm moving to Atlanta."

"If you don't mind my asking, why Atlanta, especially if New Orleans is so beautiful? Why do you want to leave?" His soothing voice probed further.

Eleanor shrugged. She thought about her

mother. "No special reason. I've decided to live in Atlanta. I visited there once with my mother. It's simply divine."

"I'm surprised Twyla hasn't tried to convince you to move to our fair city."

She laughed, relieved he didn't appear to notice her sudden mood change. "Oh, she has."

Winston was an extremely handsome man, his magnetism strong. Casting her eyes downward, she murmured, "I guess I should return to the house. I'm sure Twyla and her parents are probably wondering where I've disappeared to."

"I'll escort you back." He grabbed her hand without preamble and laid it over his arm.

Without a word, Eleanor allowed him to usher her back to the house.

Mildred was standing near the door when they returned. She awarded Eleanor with a smile that never reached her eyes. Laying a gloved hand on her son, she asked, "Winston, dear, where have you been? We've been looking all over for you."

"I needed to get some air, Mother."

It was obvious to Eleanor that he was annoyed. She moved to step around them. Before leaving, she paused to say, "Thank you for escorting me back."

Mildred waited until Eleanor was gone before speaking in a loud whisper. "It doesn't look right for you to spend all of your time with Miss Toussaint, dear. She's not your equal."

He was aghast. "You don't know anything about her, Mother."

With a wave of her hand, she brushed away his words as if they were nothing but bothersome insects. "I *do* know that she's not one of us. That's enough. Why don't you go over and rescue Jane? I don't think you two have danced all evening. Jane would make the perfect wife—"

"Do not start this again, Mother," he warned.

"Be a dear, won't you?"

Winston stopped himself from snapping out an order to stop interfering. He knew it wouldn't do any good anyway.

He walked away and headed back into the ballroom. There, Jane met him.

Eleanor watched Winston as he walked in smooth strides across the room. She'd felt a strong and immediate attraction to him in the garden, but she intended not to let it get out of hand. Her eyes met his mother's gaze from across the room. In them, she read the truth. The Blakemores' were a family where the amount of money you had dictated whether you were a first class, second class or worse—a third class citizen.

The distinguished Blakemores' were a rich white family who would not allow colored people into their world. It would not matter that her own lineage could be traced to a proud family of the French haute noblesse; she would still be colored in their eyes.

Twyla's voice broke through her musings. She turned around, a blank look on her face. "What?"

Coming into the guest room, Twyla climbed on the bed. "I was asking if you enjoyed yourself tonight?"

Eleanor nodded. She was sleepy and in no

mood for Twyla's non-stop chatter.

"What do you think of Winston?"

"He's very nice." Her tone was noncommittal.

"That's all?" Twyla folded her hands across her bosom. "Aren't you the least bit attracted to him?"

Eleanor laughed. "Well, I guess I am. He's an extremely attractive man."

Twyla clapped her hands together. "I knew it. I knew once you two saw each other—"

"No, Twyla," Eleanor cut her off. "His high and mighty mother has already picked out his bride to be. Mrs. Blakemore doesn't think I'm good enough for her son."

"I bet Winston doesn't feel that way. He couldn't keep his eyes off you. I almost felt sorry for that plain-faced Jane."

Eleanor wagged her finger at Twyla. "You shouldn't be so mean—it's not befitting a lady born of privilege."

The two doubled over in girlish laughter.

Chapter 25

"Eleanor, dear, there's someone here to see you," Twyla announced as she burst through the door of the library. Her voice was practically shaking with excitement.

"Who's here to see me?" She was clearly puzzled. "It's not Winston, is it?" She tried not to appear too hopeful.

Grinning, Twyla nodded. "Come on, don't keep him waiting."

Eleanor checked herself in the mirror. Pursing her lips into a displeasing line, she said, "But my hair. Oh, dear, I must look frightful."

Wearing a tickled expression, Twyla tried to reassure her. "You look beautiful, as always.

Now come on. He's waiting for you in the parlor."

Eleanor could barely contain her excitement. Winston Blakemore was here to see her. She paused just outside the parlor door. Spying one of the servants, she motioned for her. "Sabine, Mr. Blakemore is here. Could you please bring us a pot of tea and perhaps some sandwiches?"

"Yes, ma'am. Right away."

She entered the room gracefully. "Mr. Blakemore, this is a surprise."

He stood up. "Please call me Winston."

With ladylike gestures, Eleanor took a seat and smiled. "All right, Winston. As I was saying, I hadn't expected to see you today."

"I enjoyed out talk last night in the gardens and found that I wanted to know more about you. I thought perhaps we could take a ride—"

Eleanor shook her head regretfully. "It's very sweet of you to ask but I'm afraid I'm going to have to refuse."

His mouth went grim. "I see."

She could tell he clearly didn't. "Winston," Eleanor hedged. "I'm afraid I don't know you well enough to drive off with you in a car to who knows where. You must understand that I would have to get to know you much better before we do something like that. I've had Sabine fix us some tea and sandwiches and if you'd like, we can take a walk around the Hartwood estate. I would simply feel more comfortable in familiar surroundings."

"I understand. We'll take that walk after our afternoon tea."

Her lips curled into a smile. "Thank you for being a gentleman about this."

Sabine walked in carrying a tray laden with a polished silver teapot, pretty floral china and a plate of sandwiches.

Eleanor studied the broad build of the man sitting across from her. Winston intrigued her. She couldn't explain the reason why.

Finishing the last of his sandwich, he settled back into the high back chair.

"You know, Eleanor, our dear friend had this planned from the very beginning."

"Twyla?" She asked. "Do you really think so?"

Winston nodded. "From the moment she met you at school, Twyla's done nothing but talk about you. She thinks you're the perfect woman for me."

"And what do you think?"

His boyish grin appeared. "I can see this comes as no shock to you."

"Twyla's talked of you and I meeting many times."

His gaze traveled over her face and seemed to search her eyes. "She was right though. You are very beautiful."

The underlying sensuality of his words captivated her, sending waves of excitement through her. Blushing, Eleanor looked away. "You're very kind."

Picking up her cup, she pretended to be interested in sipping her tea.

"I think we should do as Twyla wishes. We should at least get to know one another."

Eleanor rewarded him with a radiant smile. "I see no harm in doing so."

After tea, Winston and Eleanor strolled toward the Hartwood's garden. She carried a parasol in one hand and a silk bag containing a clean handkerchief.

"We're lucky to have such good weather, don't you think? Since I've been here, it's been so hot." She gazed up at his handsome face, her insides tingling.

Winston nodded. "It's been like this the last couple of years. Real hot."

They stopped beside the lake so Eleanor could pick wild flowers.

He dropped down underneath a towering oak tree to watch her.

Catching his eyes on her, Eleanor grinned and crooked her finger. "Come here."

He stood up and mumbled, "with pleasure."

She found it exciting, the tension racing between them. Her lips ached to be kissed... Eleanor shook herself mentally.

I shouldn't be thinking of such things.

Unable to resist, Winston gently caressed her face. "You have such exquisite skin."

Eleanor closed her eyes to the feel of his hand as he gave her face a soft stroking, scalding her senses. She wondered if he, too, could feel the fire that was building between the two of them. When Winston finally removed his hand, she could still feel the heat of his touch.

"Twyla tells me you've decided not to join the family business. You're going to be a lawyer instead."

He nodded. "I have no desire to do anything but law."

"I find that an admirable occupation."

Holding held out his arm to her, he said, "Regretfully, I should return you to the safety of the house. I have an appointment that I can't miss."

Eleanor shook her head. "I don't want to leave just yet. I think I'll stay for a little while longer. I love it out here."

Winston's voice was husky. "I should like to see you again. Very soon."

She waited to speak until her quickened pulse had quieted. "I look forward to it."

Eleanor watched his quick, confident strides across the lawn. She was still watching him as he drove away.

Ten months later, Eleanor and Winston stood in front of a pastor who had agreed to marry them on short notice.

His mother was clear in her disapproval of his relationship with her, so Winston decided they should elope. He was almost finished with law school. With the money his grandparents left him, Winston purchased their first home.

Mildred Blakemore was furious when she found out, while her husband appeared to be more accepting of the marriage.

Eleanor wasn't bothered by her mother-in-law's anger. She focused on being the best wife she could to Winston.

A year after their marriage, Eleanor gave birth to a son, Winston IV. She couldn't contain her joy when she the infant came out looking white. She had worried that her tainted blood would show in her child.

Eleanor decided that she would not tempt fate by having more children. It was yet another secret she kept from her husband.

Eleanor opened her eyes.

"Oh, thank the Lord," she heard Myra say. For a moment she thought she had to be dreaming, but the beeping on a machine caught her attention. She was in a hospital.

She could hear her sister calling for a nurse. A team of nurses and two doctors soon attended to her while Myra hung around in the background and out of the way.

Their gazes met and held for a moment.

Eleanor answered a series of questions, but her eyes kept straying to her sister. She was still trying to remember how she came to be in the hospital.

"You were in a car accident," the doctor told her.

She winced when the memory rushed to the forefront of her mind. "I remember it now."

When they were alone, Myra said, "I'm so glad to see those beautiful eyes of yours. We have been keeping you lifted in prayer."

"Thank you," Eleanor said. "I'm glad to be here."

"I was so worried we were going to lose you."

"Where's Winston?"

"He's in court, but he'll be here as soon as he can."

Eleanor wet her lips. "The first time I saw you after I moved back to New Orleans, all I could think about was Mama. You look so much like her. All of the memories I'd worked hard to forget… they came running back that day, bringing with them the pain of losing her right before my very own eyes. I had it in my mind that it was because she had married a black man. Her own family disowned her. I blamed our daddy. He'd ruined what could've been a wonderful life for her because he had black skin." Tears filled her eyes. "She killed herself, Myra. She did it right in front of me."

"I'm so sorry you had to see something like that."

"I had to get out of there, so I took all the money I could find, the pearls, and I ran… I took a bus to Baton Rouge."

Myra took Eleanor's hand in her own. "For a long time, I believed someone had murdered her. Granny didn't tell me different. I thought you'd been kidnapped."

"Mama was never right after Daddy was murdered. I don't know if you know this, but she was with him the night he died."

Myra shook her head sadly. "I was born that night."

"She never got over that."

"I couldn't understand why you wanted to be *white*, but I think I do now. You witnessed something horrible and you were scared."

"I was tired of people calling me a *wan-nabe black girl.* None of the white girls wanted anything to do with me because I was taint-ed—black girls thought I was too white to be around them. People called our mama a slut because she was married to a black man. I just wanted to wash it all away."

"Honey, I had some of those same experi-ences, but after Mama died, Granny raised me and she made sure I knew our history. She told me all about Ziraili. At one time, I think you called out her name."

Eleanor felt a chill at the mention of her ancestor's name. "I don't know how to really explain it, but I kept hearing you talking to me. And there were these vivid memories of Ziraili, Nellie, Sybil, Isabel… even you and Granny." She didn't really know how to articulate what had happened to her because she wasn't exactly sure herself.

Eleanor met her sister's gaze. "I'm so sorry for the way I treated you. Please forgive me."

Myra reached over and took her hand in hers. "Only if you're willing to forgive me, too."

"I appreciate your being here with me. I heard one of the nurses say that you never left the hospital or my side for more than an hour at a time." Eleanor put a hand to her head. "How did you know I was even in the hospital? I know Winston couldn't have called you."

"My granddaughter collapsed the same day you were in that accident. I was here to see her and I saw the news that you'd been in a car accident and was in critical condition."

"Winston and I... we had dinner and on the way home..." she shook away the memory. "Is he..."

"He's just fine, Eleanor. Just fine."

"Has he been here to see me?"

Myra nodded.

"What aren't you telling me?"

"He knows the truth, Eleanor. I had to tell him because he was gonna try to keep me from seeing you."

"How did he take it?"

"He got a little indignant about the whole thing, but he didn't have no right."

Eleanor eyed her sister. "Why do you say that? He's my husband and I deceived him."

"He's done a lot of deceiving on his part as well," Myra uttered. "Eleanor, he's been having an affair with the District Attorney."

She frowned. "The black woman?"

Myra nodded. "I caught them hugged up in his hospital room. I'm sorry, but you need to know the truth."

"I can't deal with this right now. I need to focus on getting out of this hospital."

Chapter 26

Myra and Eleanor walked slowly around the park area behind the hospital. Spending so much time in bed had weakened Eleanor quite a bit, so she worked hard to regain her strength with the help of a physical therapist. She was now strong enough to take walks with her sister.

"I hope this doesn't sound crazy," Eleanor began, "but there's a part of me that believes what I experienced wasn't a dream at all."

Myra smiled. "Maybe it wasn't."

Eleanor gave her a summary of what happened while she was in the coma.

Her words made Myra shudder. "Honey, I don't know if it's because I was talking about those things—all I know is that I just had a chill run down my spine."

"It seems so real. I know things about the past that I never knew before. How do I begin to make sense of all this?"

"I don't know," Myra responded. "Our family has gone though some incredible things over the years."

"But what do you believe?" Eleanor asked. "Do you think it's possible that I *actually* experienced everything I just told you?"

"Yes," Myra said. "I believe it because Ziraili came to me once."

Eleanor gasped in surprise. "When?"

"The day of Mama's funeral. I was upstairs in one of the bedrooms. She wrapped me in her arms and told me that everything was going to be fine. I looked for her at the service and asked Granny about her. That's when she showed me a picture of Ziraili. Her name means God's Helper."

"I never knew our ancestors were so brave and courageous; the women were strong despite all they had to deal with," Eleanor said. "I just wish I knew what ever happened to Sybil. Do you know?"

Myra shook her head. "No one knows."

"I suppose that will always be a gap in our history."

"You're getting stronger," Myra stated. "We walked more today than you have in the past."

"I still get tired pretty quickly," Eleanor responded.

"Then let's head back to your room."

"I'm hoping the doctor will let me go home tomorrow."

Winston was waiting for her when they returned.

"I'll leave you two to talk," Myra said.

"How are you feeling?" he asked.

"Much better," Eleanor replied as she sat on the bed. "I spoke with our son earlier. He's upset that you didn't tell him about the accident or that I was in a coma."

"It's not like we hear from him all that often," Winston said. "I didn't want to worry him."

Their son was in the Marines and currently stationed in Afghanistan.

"Where do we go from here?" Eleanor asked. "There are no more secrets between us. You know I have African American blood running through my veins; I know that you've been cheating on me with Janet—I know about the girl in Baton Rouge, too."

"We've been together a long time," Winston said. "I do love you, Eleanor. I felt like we were drifting apart. It's one of the reasons I decided to move here. I thought being back in New Orleans would make you happy."

"You did this for me?"

Winston nodded. "Yes, but then it seemed to only make you sadder. Now I understand why."

"My lineage is no longer a secret."

"I know and I'm okay with it."

"Are you sure?"

"Yes. I want you and I want our marriage."

"What about—"

"It's over," Winston said. "She's not worth losing you over."

"I have to be honest with you," Eleanor told him. "I'm not sure what I want right now. A lot has happened. My main focus is to make sure I'm healthy. The rest I'll deal with one day at a time."

"I'm not going to give up on us."

"Then why was Myra the one constantly by

my bedside in the hospital?" Eleanor asked.

"I felt like she would be able to reach you better than I could."

Winston said down beside her. "A part of me was ashamed, Eleanor. I was embarrassed that Myra had caught me with Janet. I know she doesn't think much of me."

"You didn't give her much to like about you. To be honest, I'm not sure how I feel about you right now."

"I'll do whatever I have to do to gain your trust back."

"Winston, I am going to need some time."

"I can give you that."

6 Months Later

Belva and Vincent walked out of the doctor's office smiling.

Both Julia and Myra stood up.

"God is good," Belva stated. "There are no signs of the disease. I'm in remission."

"Hallelujah," Myra said. "Girl, I just want to start shouting up in here, but I'll wait until

I get home."

"Praise party at Nana's house," Belva said with a chuckle. "I'm right there with you."

Everyone gathered at Myra's house to celebrate.

She turned on a Gospel music station and began dancing. Belva and Vincent joined her in the middle of the living room floor, singing and giving praise to God.

Fanning herself with her hand, Myra sank down on the sofa. "Oooh... thank you, Lord."

The doorbell sounded.

"I'll get it," Julia said as she came down the stairs.

She came to the living room with Eleanor in tow.

Myra was surprised to see her sister. Normally, she saw Eleanor at her home. This was the third time her sister had come to this house.

"Hey Sister," Myra greeted.

"You all look cheerful."

"I'm in remission, Aunt Eleanor," Belva announced.

Eleanor sat down beside Myra. "That's wonderful news."

Everyone left the room, leaving Myra alone

with her sister.

"How are things going with you and Winston?"

"I'm still not sure if I'm going to stay in the marriage," Eleanor confessed. "He's the only man I've ever loved, but I'm not sure I'll ever be able to trust him again."

"You'll do what's right for you."

"I brought the photo albums back. They're in the foyer," Eleanor said. "It was so surreal for me because I recognized them. Myra, I knew exactly who they were without turning the picture over to see the name. I feel like I've known them forever."

She pulled a velvet pouch out of her purse. "The reason I came by is to bring you these, Myra. You're right, they belong with the Toussaint family."

Myra fingered the pearls. "They're beautiful." She glanced at her sister. "Eleanor, thank you, but you should keep them. I'd like for Belva to wear them for her wedding though."

"Every woman in our family will wear them on her wedding day, going forward," Eleanor said. "I will keep them for now, but when I'm gone, I want them to come to you."

Myra grinned. "I made Granny's lemon pound cake. Would you like a piece?"

"I'm not leaving here without having some."

Eleanor followed her sister into the kitchen. "You're going to have to give me the recipe."

"Move out of the way and let Nana through the door," Belva ordered.

Gathering up the yards of fabric that made up her wedding dress, she stepped out of the way as her grandmother strolled into the medium-sized dressing room. She tossed her bridal veil to the side as she leaned down to place a kiss on the woman's cheek.

Her bridesmaids quickly left the room to give them some privacy.

Taking a soft sponge, Belva lightly blended the ivory-tinted foundation Myra wore into her skin. "You look real pretty, Nana."

"It's a beautiful day for a wedding, dear. Just beautiful."

Belva turned to face the oak full-length mirror running her hands up and down her beaded gown. "What do you think, Nana?"

"I think you make a beautiful bride." Myra's eyes teared up. "You remind me so much of your mother when she was your age. The pearls look stunning with your dress."

"It was so nice of Eleanor to let me wear them."

Myra nodded. "It's been nice having my sister back in my life. We even had our first argument last week."

Belva laughed. "About what, Nana?"

"How to make Granny's homemade biscuits."

"I guess she decided to stay married to Winston."

"Yeah," Myra said. "They have been together over 40 years. She might as well stay with him."

"I wish Granddaddy was here."

"Me, too, sugar. I miss him so much." Myra planted a kiss on Belva's cheek. "I'd better get inside. The ceremony will be starting soon. I'm so happy for you, love."

In the sanctuary, Myra was escorted to the front pew. Before she took her seat, Myra silently acknowledged her six grandchildren sitting on the second row with a slight wave.

The pianist began to play softly, while people continued filtering into the large room, spilling onto seats all around. Myra moved her head to the music as she tapped her toe to its rhythm.

Tears of joy welled up in her eyes. She had lived long enough to witness the wedding ceremony of her oldest grandchild. Myra sent up a silent prayer of thanksgiving.

Someone offered her a tissue.

Grateful, she looked up into blue eyes that matched her own. She could feel the heat of everyone's eyes on them and tilted her chin upward. "Sit with me, Eleanor."

"Thank you. I wasn't sure where I—"

"You're my sister, Eleanor." Myra interjected while gently dabbing at her eyes. "I'm glad you decided to come."

Eleanor glanced over at her. "It sure doesn't take long for news to travel around this town. People are staring us down. Outside, when I walked up, the crowd parted like the Red Sea."

Myra chuckled. "Pay them no mind. Belva's going to be thrilled that you're here."

"And you?"

"I'm real happy, Eleanor. I've dreamed of

this day for a long time."

"I feel like I've finally come home. It's like my life has been on pause all these years. I can't fully explain it."

"Sometimes you have to look back before you can move forward." Myra reached over and took her sister's hand. "My problem was that I spent too much time looking backward that I couldn't move on." She smiled. "I think we got it right this time."

Chapter 27

"Remember I told you that I had a surprise for you," Julia stated, a couple of days after Belva's wedding.

Myra nodded while Eleanor was curious about the two white women standing beside her niece.

"Remember how we have always wondered what happened that night Sybil disappeared and if she ever made it up north?"

Eleanor and Myra exchanged curious glances.

Julia broke into a smile. "Well, these two women are descendants of Sybil."

Myra gazed at them and said, "Our Sybil?"

Julia introduced Lila and Claire to her mother and Eleanor.

"Well, I'll be…" Myra uttered. "I guess we're about to find out."

They settled in the living room.

Lila spoke first. "Our mother passed away last month. Claire and I were going through some of her things because we're planning to sell the house. While unpacking some of her boxes in the attic, we found a journal that belonged to Sybil."

"Oh, so you're not related to her," Eleanor said.

"Sybil was our great, great, great-grandmother. She came up north to Canada after she left the Gerard Plantation. She wrote about losing her daughter Molly when she was just a child; about Josiah being sold and how the slave owner betrayed her when he sold Sam. I hope that we don't offend you by saying this, but we never knew that we… that she was a slave. I don't think anyone in our family knew."

"Sybil married a white man," Lila announced. "We believe that because she was so light—it was easy for her to pass."

Eleanor nodded in understanding. "She was very light-skinned and had long light brown hair that was very straight."

Myra and Julia glanced over at her in surprise.

Claire handed them some pictures. "This is Sybil and her husband on their wedding day."

"Does the journal speak of how she escaped?" Eleanor asked.

Lila and Claire both nodded, but it was Lila who said, "Sybil and her companions didn't get too far before they were discovered by a slave catcher. One of the men died, but the other got away. The slave catcher had cornered Sybil and was about to rape her when he was attacked."

Eleanor felt the hair on the back of her neck stand up. "Did she say who attacked him?"

"Yes, she said it was Ziraili, her grandmother."

Myra gasped in surprise, and then glanced over at Eleanor.

"So, let me get this straight," Julia said. "A woman she thought was Ziraili saved her—only Ziraili has been dead for many years by then. Sybil got away, made it up north and then started passing for white?"

Lila and Claire nodded.

"How did you find us?"

"We found Sam. Found out that his daughter Sophie and her children went up to Canada."

"The children belonged to her sister Ruth Anne—she died shortly after Gemma was born," Eleanor interjected. "Sophie raised them as her own."

"We didn't know that," Claire stated. "We just assumed they were Sophie's children. Anyway, we found that Gemma left Canada and moved to New Orleans. From there, we were eventually led to Myra. It was Sybil's final wish to have her family reunited and that's why we came here. We wanted to honor her wishes, but also to meet the rest of our family."

Myra smiled. "It's always been my wish as well."

"Not everyone knows about this in our family," Claire said. "We really didn't know where to begin... we just had to come and now that we have—we're going to sit everyone down and share what Sybil wrote in her journal. It may take some of our family members a while to adjust to the truth, I hate to say."

While Myra and the women talked, Eleanor got up, walked over to the huge picture window and stared outside.

"That's incredible, don't you think?" Myra asked when she joined her.

She nodded. "Sybil's descendants. Wow."

"They haven't fainted from the shock of black relatives. I'm impressed," Myra said with a chuckle.

"They seem really nice," Eleanor responded. "I like them."

Myra wrapped an arm around her. "So, do I."

Julia announced that dinner was ready.

Eleanor followed her sister and the others into the dining room.

Nearing the doorway, she felt like someone was watching her and turned around, catching sight of a tall dark-skinned woman outside the window who gave her a big smile, before vanishing right before her eyes.

Ziraili.

CPSIA information can be obtained
at www.ICGtesting.com
Printed in the USA
LVOW10s0118260417
532192LV00007B/97/P